IT WAS

YOU

By

Jade Lee Wright

Dedication

This book is dedicated to my family and friends who have always supported me, read my drafts and offered me constructive criticism and feedback. I couldn't have gotten this book to where it is today without all of your help. You know who you are.
Thank you.

Jade Lee Wright is a book reviewer, writer, podcaster and bookstagrammer born in England. She grew up in a small scenic town in South Africa and now lives in Brisbane, Australia with her partner who she is eagerly pestering to get cats and dogs to grow their family and home!

She has a bookish podcast called Books & Booze where she gets to chat about books (predominantly her love of thriller novels) and interview authors!

She is currently working on her second thriller novel.

Follow all of her bookish adventures on Instagram:
@boho_bookworm / @booksboozepod

Prologue

The door to the coffee shop yawns open.

Peyton's eyes swivel in their sockets until she finds me in an alcove across the foyer.

With cautious steps she hurries towards me.

African music pulses through the pinewood walls. A group of performers play bongo drums and wooden horn bell trumpets, telling a story through their dance and chants out on the sidewalk. Tendons and delicate twig like bones move frantically around in her hands as she clutches onto the pot of burnt coffee that I've already ordered.

The table wobbles as we fidget in our seats, neither one of us wanting to be the first to speak. Peyton, harboring onto her fear, takes the wooden menu in her hands even though we both know we won't be ordering food.

She hides behind it and I stare at the globs of congealed glue coating the sides until a waitress comes over to us. Her name badge reads Princess. It's a typical name among the Africans. Peyton and I would usually joke about it, but today is different.

We turn down the waitress's suggestion to try a slice of the cafes freshly baked Malva pudding drenched in hot custard.

The moment Peyton had walked through the door I'd lost my appetite. She looks disheveled, undone. It's so unlike her usual self. I've never seen her look so weak. Vulnerable.

Whatever this is, it's bad.

We met on the beach over ten years ago.

I'd been out on one of my melancholy walks when this flamboyant, dark-skinned woman bounded up to me with a trail of impossibly long corkscrew curls behind her.

She'd given me the most startlingly large smile I'd ever seen, holding out her camera and asking me to take a picture for her.

I'd fumbled with her camera and nodded politely. I couldn't really say no, could I?

I'd watched as she darted to her left, grabbing ahold of a young girl with an identical mop of pitch black hair.

"Smile, Harley!" the woman crooned into the girl's ear, squeezing her sides to force out a giggling yelp.

They fell into each other, laughing and playing and I wasn't sure if I should wait until they calmed down or start snapping away.

I chose the latter.

I smiled as I took photograph after photograph; although it felt like I was watching something intimate that I wasn't supposed to be a part of.

The woman was gasping for breath as I handed the camera back to her.

"Are you a photographer?" she had asked me, flicking through the photographs.

I remember blushing then, enjoying the feeling of the compliment.

I shook my head, though I wished I could have said yes.

A part of me had wanted to lie and seem more interesting.

I wanted her to like me.

She smiled at me again.

"Well, you should be."

Her smile was captivating. I couldn't look away.

"I'm Peyton and this-" she pointed her thumb across to the small girl who instantly interrupted her.

"Harley!" The girl said with a self-assured voice that I don't think I've ever heard from someone so young. She was admiringly assertive for someone who must have been no more than three years old.

She commanded attention.

Peyton and Harley stared at me with indistinguishable grins.

It was almost as though they were in competition with each other.

"I'm Regan," I mumbled, my voice barely audible above the sound of the ocean.

I'd always been socially dislocated with my anxiety and unremarkable features but I remember feeling strangely shy in front of them; particularly the little girl.

Kids had always made me feel uncomfortable. I wasn't good with them.

I think they sensed my desire for approval and used it to their advantage.

Peyton and I had fallen into conversation as we walked back along the beach together, Harley charging ahead of us splashing in the waves.

She seemed oblivious to this third party who had shown up during her time on the beach with her mother.

I think I preferred that I felt invisible around her.

From that day on Peyton had taken me under her wing and we'd remained friends ever since. Opposites attract, as they say.

"What's happened?" I ask her now, staring at her nicotine stained fingers that match our ochre yellow mugs.

Her fingers are swollen from pregnancy.

Skirting around the question, Peyton beckons the waitress back over.

She hasn't said a word since sitting down at the table.

I stare at her aging features as she orders Rooibos tea, her words come out mangled.

"Peyton, speak to me!" I say imploringly, reaching out to touch her hand. It's trembling.

She flinches away from me, making my thoughts ricochet around the room.

"Has someone hurt you?"

She shakes her head, leaching out the last of my patience.

Her lips part; her strong jaw quivering as she searches for the right words.

We both jump as her phone vibrates violently, skittering across the tabletop.

All of the courage she's been summoning evaporates.

Harley's face flashes up onto the screen. We stare at it for a moment too long; wide grin and sharp white teeth stealing the rest of the photograph.

She has a light dusting of freckles over her well defined nose and high cheek bones.

"I need to get this..." she whispers. Her voice is strangulated.

She lifts herself up on shaky legs and starts to walk back towards the entrance.

I thrum my knuckles on the table. Rat-tat-tat.

"Hi, sweetie," I hear her say into the phone. Her voice instantly sugars.

I watch her pace back and forth through the coffee shop window while she speaks to her daughter. She looks harried, like she's trying to explain herself.

I sip at my coffee, waiting.

When she returns, she's even more flustered than before.

The chair creaks under her weight as she sits back down.

A coffee machine screams in the corner of the room.

"It's Harley," she eventually says through gritted teeth.

I remain silent, watching her thumb the screen of her phone until she places it to one side.

She looks up at me reluctantly.

"I'm scared, Regan. I don't even know how to say this without sounding completely crazy."

"Try," I encourage her carefully.

I can hear a clock from somewhere in the room while the performers outside thank someone for putting a handful of coins into their shabby hat.

Tick. Tock.

"She doesn't want me to have Nova."

There's no mistaking the fear in her eyes as she places her hands over her eight month baby bump.

Without even thinking about it, I tell her that's ridiculous.

It has to be.

It's such a fallacious thing to say that I'd laugh if it weren't for how unequivocally petrified she looks.

"I'm serious. She keeps doing all these weird things. Trashing the nursery, throwing out the new baby albums I bought. After the baby shower she tried to take all of the presents back to the stores."

"It sounds like she's just acting out, P. She'll come around to it."

I'm trying to sound like I know what I'm talking about but the truth is, I'm the youngest child myself and have no idea what it's like to have another baby come in and take my parents away from me.

Not that I really had much parenting to begin with, anyway.

"It's not just that, there are other things too. She says I don't need the baby things because I'm not having a baby. It's like she refuses to accept it. When I told her the baby was kicking the other day she put her hands over my stomach and when Nova kicked, Harley pushed back hard, really hard. It scared me a lot, Regan."

There are tears in her eyes.

I consider this for a moment.

I guess I'm trying to be pragmatic.

The feeling of babies kicking inside the womb freaks me out, too.
Maybe that's why Harley reacted that way. Peyton doesn't give me
a chance to respond.

"I don't know if she's going to be able to handle not being the
center of attention."

It's true that for thirteen years, she has always been the epicenter
of her mother's universe.

I don't know what to say.

"She's so angry. I honestly just don't know what she's capable of
right now!"

I clear my throat, sipping on the welcomed bitterness of black
coffee.

"I think there are a lot of hormones in your house right now. You
need to remember she's thirteen. Teenage hormones plus your
pregnancy hormones is *going* to be a lethal combination."

She sighs, nodding forlornly before choking back a sob.

"I'm the worst mother in the world!"

"No you aren't," I say, meaning it.

"Regan, I'm scared of my own daughter..." her sparkling eyes bleed
right into mine, making the hair stand up on my arms.

We finish our drinks in silence, neither one of us knowing what to say.

When the bill comes we have our usual fuss over who's going to settle the tab. As always, Peyton wins. She's always had a much stronger personality than I ever will.

When the change is brought over I watch Peyton ferret it away. She is still on edge.

I shrug on my mottled blazer as we begin our procession down the coffee shop steps. The bricks are cracked and loose beneath our feet.

There's an Autumnal nip in the air and the usual scent of cooking oil lingering in the breeze.

The first thing she does when we're out on the sidewalk is light a cigarette. The smoke blows back into my face but for once I don't care. Passersby shoot her filthy looks, their eyes flitting between the cigarette and her bulging stomach. She doesn't seem to notice. I've become fairly used to receiving looks from strangers whenever I'm around Peyton. She has the rare ability to not give a shit about what anyone thinks of her. From her tumultuous voice to her animated personality, she always remained true to herself and I've always been enamored by her.

I think that's why it shakes me so much to see her as run down as she is right now.

"Hey, you're going to be OK," I assure her, placing a hand on her arm as she unlocks her car.

A boy wearing a dirty, hole-filled shirt that must have once been white comes running over to us to let us know that her car is still ok. No one had tried to smash the windows and steal it today.
I smile at him gratefully and hand him a silver coin.
He looks down at it in the palm of his hand and grins as though he is now rich. He runs off to show his group of barefooted friends who are staring at us eagerly.
Peyton pivots towards me, throwing her arms around my neck and almost knocking me off balance. She smells like she always does. Caramel perfume, too sweet for me, mixed with cigarette smoke. It's a smell I've come to love. I breathe her in, feeling her curls whip around us in the wind.

I can't shake an unsettling feeling as I hug her back a little too tightly.

I should have paid more attention.

1

One Week Earlier

The wheels of my suitcase scrape along the concrete as I tug it up my parent's driveway.

As the battered front door comes into view a feeling of weight descends down onto my shoulders.

The house, even from the outside looking in, feels sad.

The rusted gate that has been a fixture of our family home since the day we bought it swings in the breeze. Beside it, hung up by a loose nail, is a chipped wooden board with the words *'Welcome Home'* in faded blue paint. The irony is almost too much for me.

The house hasn't changed a bit. The rose bushes my mother had once tended to like they were her children are still scorched from the hot African sun.

The soil dry and hard, unloved.

The hole dad had started digging near the aloe plants to the right of the property hasn't seemed to progress at all.

I've never known what that hole was for.

The place looks run down; with windows so dirty you can barely see through them. Some are shattered, shards of glass coating the ground.

This place has never felt like 'home'.

Memories flood to the forefront of my mind, eager to make their presence known.

I don't welcome them back.

They're watching me from the window, their Jack Russell squealing inconsolably at my arrival.

Her voice box clearly hadn't been damaged when she'd swallowed that fishhook last year.

I clench my jaw as the front door groans open, begging for oil. It reveals my mother in her usual ensemble of tracksuit pants and an oversized shirt.

Her usual shock of dyed red hair is faded and frazzled.

She looks horrific. The stench of stale alcohol clings desperately onto her as she lurches forward, drawing me into a clumsy embrace. I close my eyes, willing myself not to cry. Spittle from her thinned lips soaks my shoulder.

I'd been told to brace myself but nothing can prepare you for this. The drinking has thinned her blood so much that her arms are covered in bruise like marks of broken blood vessels. Her skin has drooped and become riddled with liver spots that she is too young to have. Her eyes which had always been too dark to make out the pupils have become sunken slits in their sockets. There is not an ounce of life in them anymore, they are lackluster and empty. She is half the size of me. Her leg muscles so disintegrated it makes her walk in a way that looks like she's shat herself.

Dad welcomes me with an awkward pat on the back. Age has softened him, I notice as he hefts my luggage inside.

A coffee table in the middle of the lounge is barely recognizable beneath the dog hair, dried muddy paw prints, nail clippings, dust and pill packets to control my mother's seizures.

I wonder for a moment as I look around the tip of a room when they had let the maid go or if she had simply walked out on them. I know I would have.

We all walk into my old bedroom, a heavy wave of nostalgia crashes through me as I look around. They've done it up nicely for me; made the bed, placed a vase with an array of brightly colored flowers on the bedside table; pincushion proteas, arum-lilies and blood red roses (clearly not from their garden). They smell strong, giving me an instant migraine.

I thank them in a low voice, my cheeks ablaze.

I can't stand this feeling, the feeling of needing them.

I've never needed anyone before so the relief of having my family and friends so close by after so many years away is foreign to me. "I'll start looking for a place of my own tomorrow," I tell them, fixing my bloodshot eyes on the cobwebs in the corner of my windowsill. Cleaning rich bastards' yachts over the last couple of years has turned me into someone that no one who'd previously known me would recognize. I wasn't the same anymore.

"You can stay as long as you like. We're happy to have you home," dad says, giving me one of his smiles that say he feels sorry for me. Mum's hair bounces up and down on her bony shoulders as she nods her agreement. I sigh.

"Thank you."

They leave the room, shutting the door gently behind them.

I am left alone in a strange silence that I should be used to by now.

My gaze falls to a patch of paint on the wall that didn't quite match the rest; a touch up from a recent dent made by a fist.

Dad's fist.

Better the wall than my mother's body, I think queasily.

I hate thinking it, but I can't help but understand his frustration.

I'd want to punch through walls if I had to live with her, too.

Having a mother that far gone with alcoholism is impossible to explain to someone if they aren't in the same situation.

You feel so ungrateful for despising them because so many people have lost their mothers and would do anything to have just one more day with them.

I avoid my mother like the plague and although I hate to admit it, there are times where I think it would be easier if she were dead.

It disgusts me to know that if this woman who had carried me in her womb for nine months, raised me and loved me and had become my best friend were to draw her last breath I would feel relief.

What kind of daughter feels that way?

There had been years of trying to help her, coax her into going to rehab, removing all of the alcohol from the house and challenging the entire family to take part in 'Sober October.'

All to no avail.

The second we would go out as a family to a restaurant, the sommelier would come over and ruin everything but it was never really the sommelier's fault, was it?

I used to hate that saying, 'You can't help someone if they won't help themselves.'

I guess I never understood it until now, in my late twenties as I watch my mother slipping away right before my eyes.

It's like watching your mother dying of cancer.

She is deteriorating, balding, weakening... but unlike cancer, this is her choice.

Granted cancer and alcoholism are both diseases and once the latter has you in its clutches, it won't let you go. But she still chose to pick up that bottle in the first place.

I keep thinking that there must have been a moment when she realized that what she was doing was dangerous.

There must have come a time when she was busy burying a box of wine under her shoes so that no one else could find it or see it and thought to herself, 'this is bad.' Surely?

Where is the turning point?

I drink alone sometimes.

I love cooking with a glass of red in my hand and I can admit that if I have a bad day I do turn to a drink for comfort.

I wonder then if I am heading in her direction.

Do other people do that? Drink alone at night?

I don't have enough to make me drunk, just enough to feel lighter. Not enough to forget, but enough to feel like that's a possibility down the track.

I shake my thoughts away before they fester.

I look reluctantly at my suitcase, filled with my life from the past few years. It's crammed with books mainly.

I wasn't able to bring everything that I'd wanted back with me from the house I shared with my ex in Spain.

I'm not ready to unzip it yet, something about doing that would make it seem all the more real when right now it still feels like I'm in some obscure universe.

Nothing feels right.

I sit on the lumpy bed and press my fingertip into a thorn from the stem of a rose.

Mesmerized, I watch blood trickle down from the palm of my hand onto my wrist.

I am completely entranced until my phone beeps.

I didn't even have to look before knowing that it's from him.

No one else has my new Spanish number. Not since he smashed my old phone and snapped my sim-card in half.

Hello Guapa. Are you home safe?

His message disarms me instantly. *Guapa.* I used to love it when he called me that. It had been 'our thing' when I'd started learning Spanish for him. I'd reciprocate with '*Hello Guapo,*' and we'd smile at how the word sounded through my British accent.

It had gone from Guapa to *Amore.* He didn't call me *that* anymore. How could he text me something so *normal* after what he'd done? I'm infuriated.

The childish part of me wants to send him a stack of 'Fuck You's' in return but I swallow back my temper. It goes down like knives.

I know I should block him, remove any trace of him from my life – let my battered heart and the bruises scattered across my body heal and slowly forget about him, but I have to wean myself off of him slowly. I'm also waiting for an apology.

It's all I want, acknowledgement for what he's done… and honestly, I don't know how to let him go yet. Not fully.

Leaving Spain was been the biggest and hardest decision of my life because regardless of what he'd done, I was still in love with him.

I am in love with him.

I hate that I am.

I hate that I love someone who has disrespected me for so many years of my life, cheating on me with over eight women and abusing me both physically and verbally.

I've never felt more ashamed of myself. Ashamed that I can't control my feelings for him and ashamed because I feel so worthless when deep down I know *he* is the worthless one. But love doesn't just disappear.

As much as I hate him, those feelings still remain. It's the most contradicting, confusing feelings I've ever had and all I want to do is sleep for eternity. But life doesn't stop so neither can I.

◊

It doesn't take me long to find a flat just off of the main road, past an old sign pointing to a rifle range. It's a cozy two-bedroomed, fully furnished wooden cottage with a small overgrown garden, dark green fencing and bars in front of the windows. It even has a fireplace inside and a porch out front that I can't wait to use while reading my book in the sun. Even though I've seen the figures increasing in my bank account for the past few years, it still stuns me that I was able to pay for the place six months upfront. Having this much money is very new to me. It'll get me by for a while at least.

My new landlord, a frumpy old woman covered in cat hair, told me that I could move in immediately which I was more than happy about.

Staying in such close proximity to my mother just wasn't a good idea.

My first evening in the cottage feels surreal.

I feel like I'm house-sitting for someone.

Nothing feels like mine because everything from the mattress on the floor to the beige sofa crammed into the dusty corner belongs to my landlord. It's so different to the home I had created for Sean and me in Spain.

The artwork on the walls is no longer the memorable photographs I'd taken of a set of waves rolling into Jeffrey's Bay, South Africa.

Something to remind us of home while in Spain. They are replaced in this new, unfamiliar place with a triptych of black and white shots. An unknown lighthouse surrounded by a raging murky sea. The panels unsettle me. I tear myself away from them eventually and creep into my quaint kitchen, the sagging floorboards creaking beneath me. Uncorking a bottle of wine, I splash a hearty lug into a glass I discover in one of the cupboards above the sink.

The hinges of the cupboards are rusted and whine incessantly as I open and close them, familiarizing myself with my surroundings.

I curl up into a ball with my glass of wine and create a new resumé on my laptop, listening to the sound of my fingertips hitting the keyboard.

Try to sell yourself more, people had always advised me.

You've done so much at such a young age, they said as though it was something to be proud of. I don't see it that way as I look at the document in front of me. I see a history of a woman who can't keep the same job for more than six months. I see someone restless, noncommittal. I've never really known what it is that I want to do with my life and it sure as hell hadn't been my latest stint on the yachts but I'd done it for *him*.

I finish it up and read through the brief history of my life, realizing that it doesn't really seem like mine. I can barely remember the days of becoming best friends with office fax machines and printers, having stacks of papers taller than I was to file away, being a circuit coach at Curves International or selling art for one of the most respected, eccentric artists in South Africa. Had this really been my life? I take a sip of my wine as I mull this over in my head.

I'm grateful when I come across an old CD player with a selection of albums from artists I gather are from the Fifties or Sixties piled alongside it.

I slot in a CD from one of the only bands I actually know, The Beatles. The sides of my mouth tug up into a small smile as Here Comes The Sun fills the room and before I know it I'm swaying my hips along to the music, sipping my wine as I circle my new living quarters.

I've been so uncertain about where life has taken me, but in this moment, listening to this song, it feels like everything really is alright.

When the song strums to an end I'm out of breath and my small smile has spread from ear to ear. My cheeks are hot from the alcohol and my head feels light. I laugh, feeling stupid even though I know no one can see me.

I stop in front of my fireplace and crouch down with a firelighter wedged between my thumb and forefinger. The room is soon emblazoned with an orange glow. I switch off the music to listen to the sound of the crackling fire. I'm sitting cross-legged on the floor warming my bones besides the flames when I hear a thump. My heart rate skyrockets as I fly to my feet and look wildly around the room, the blade of my nose flying this way and that. The first thought to enter my head is, 'how did he find me?' I realize then that it won't be as easy as I'd envisioned to stop living in constant fear of him.

Wine sloshes out of the glass that is firmly grasped in my hand, landing on the floor. It leaves an angry red stain instantly, making my mind suddenly switch over to my deposit rather than the unknown noise. I scurry over to the sink, wetting a sponge and returning to the stain to try and scrub it away with little success.

"Fuck..." I growl, tossing the sponge to the side and picking my wine glass back up to take another sip.

The same thumping noise shatters through the near silence once again, shooting a shiver up my spine. I tingle from head to toe, goose bumps scattering my forearms as I feel my nipples harden beneath my bra. My eyes, swollen and tender from crying earlier, dart madly around the room. My phone flashes at me from across the lounge. I'm too scared to move.

When a high-pitched wail reverberates through my eardrums my heart jumps into my throat. It's coming from my bathroom, behind the door I'd closed earlier in the evening. I can feel the blood pulsing through my head as I consider my options. Funnily enough, the first option, albeit unrealistic, is to call for Sean to help... the one man that I am scared of.

I try to remember the bathroom. Are there bars on the windows? If not, are the windows big enough to fit through? I can't remember. The wine has made my memory of the cottage hazy at best. Something scratches at the door, making it bash against the framing. I cling to my knees in fear. I see a wrought iron fireplace tool set, scramble across the room and seize one of the tools. Feeling the weight of it in my hand gives me courage I don't think I could have conjured up without it.

I fly towards the bathroom, letting out a baffling battle cry as I thrust open the door. A pair of shiny eyes blink up at me in the darkness giving me such a fright that I fall backwards, sending my weapon clattering to the floor.

It's small, whatever it was. I crawl carefully over to the light switch and smack my hand down onto it. Blinded by the brightness, I struggle to get my sight back for a moment, and then I see it. It has wrapped itself around my discolored shower curtain, its tail shivering in the sheer delight of being noticed. A cat. I've never liked them.

I look at my open window, bars barricade the area but somehow the cat has managed to weasel its way in. I try shooing it away in irritation but it weaves itself around my legs, leaving a layer of fur behind on my black leggings.

It purrs as soon as I swat it, its head butting into the back of my hand. I soften slightly as I caress its delicate skull with my fingers. No sooner have I done so when its eyes suddenly widen and it takes off stealthily through the gap between the burglar bars by the window.

I stand dumbfounded for a moment before dragging my feet back towards the fading fireplace. I top up the logs, grabbing my phone and unlocking the screen with my fingerprint.

Settling down onto the sofa, I feel a pang of loneliness shoot through me. I blame it on the cat. That unexpected company if only for a matter of seconds has done something to me. My heart pines for another message from Sean even though I haven't responded to any of his others. Even though his messages irritate me, a part of me still wants them.

I scroll through my contacts, their profile images appearing alongside their names on my phone. Peyton has updated her profile picture again; it's an almost daily occurrence. This time she's updated it to one that isn't even of herself. It's a photo of her daughter. I never really understood the point in putting up a photograph of someone or something else, but then again I'd never had a dog or a cat, or in her case, a child.

Harley's extravagant grin shines out at me from my phone. It's a contagious smile. She really is a beautiful child.

I start typing a message to her.

Peyton, you have the most beautiful daughter in the world!

The wine has allowed me to venture into a happier place, at least for the time being. I revel in the moment, until a ping on my phone tells me that I have a new message. I expect it to be from Peyton, so when an unknown number shows up above the text it takes me by surprise.

You're sexy.

I frown, staring at the message in confusion. The mere thought that it could be Harley is so perverse; I shake it from my head instantly. The phone pulses beside me, showing me I have another unread message. I don't want to look.

2

The messages rattled me. They kept pouring in throughout the night until I stopped opening them entirely.

I've never enjoyed parties, especially if they were for me. Peyton really outdid herself to throw me a special welcome home bash though, so I can't really refuse.

It feels nice to break away from my laptop anyway. I'm up to my teeth in job applications and have already received a handful of politely written rejections. I doubt that any of them have had the time to read my entire resumé yet. So far the responses all seem very similar.

Short and to the point, letting me know that they are pursuing candidates with more experience but promising to keep my application on record in case something more suitable comes up in the future.

Bullshit.

I crack each of my vertebras as I stare up at the house. Traipsing up her cobbled pathway, I can hear the sound of something terrible blasting from the speakers inside. Peyton flings the door open before I've even had a chance to knock and ushers me inside. It's the first time I've seen her in over a year; she looks stunning in a flowing maternity top, her wild curls clipped back out of her face.

She envelopes me in her arms and I work my way into an uncomfortable hug, her protruding belly button getting in the way. The feeling of something so alien poking me freaks me out.

"That asshole never deserved you," she says, smacking kisses into my ear which temporarily deafens me.

Everyone is already here. All the friends I'd missed so sorely while living away from home.

I never thought I'd be returning to them under these sorts of circumstances.

I never thought I'd rather not see any of them again. I want to avoid the inevitable questions; the thought of having the retell my grisly nightmare for the umpteenth time is almost too much to bear.

"How're things with your folks?" Peyton asks, holding me at arm's length. She always cuts right to the point.

"Terrible. I've inherited another child. She's called Mum," I say, my voice dripping with sarcasm.

I tell her about the messages from my mother begging me to go and buy her a five litre box of wine this morning. Dad's taken away her car keys because she's never sober enough to drive – not that that's stopped her before.

Do I feel like a bitch for joking about my mother that way? Yes. Yes I do, but it doesn't stop me.

After being passed around the room, a disembodying feeling, Harley sidles up next to me. My godchild. She emanates an unsettling excitement as she looks up at me with her elfin face.

"Tried to get her to go to a friend for the night but she said she wanted to see her Auntie Regan," Peyton says, winking at her daughter. Harley's facial expression darkens as she switches her gaze from me to her mother. There is a strange energy charging between them that's hard to miss.

I try pushing the thoughts of the weird messages I'd received to the side as I hug Harley hello.

"God, you've grown!" I say genuinely as I hold her skeletal frame in my hands.

"So have you," Harley replies, poking my stomach tantalizingly.

"Harley!" Peyton chastises. I redden.

After finding out about Sean's extracurricular activities with a handful of Spanish and Argentinian women, I'd stayed with him. I'd made myself believe that we could get through it if we worked harder on our relationship. I'd forced him to tell each woman about me, made him delete their numbers and basically grovel for my forgiveness.

Instead of our sex life dwindling, it made me want to fuck him more. Take what was rightfully mine. It had been poisonous and heart-wrenching even to me to see how desperate I became for his attention and affection.

I think the groveling had lasted all of one day before he went back to having me under his thumb.

The little self-confidence I did possess was shattered and I'd stopped eating. I hadn't realized how bad it was until I stepped onto the scale and read something terrifying. I weighed thirty-six kilograms. I hadn't noticed the shift in my body before then; not even when I'd dropped a cup size.

After that I'd started binge eating, shoveling food into my body every second of the day. I was lucky that in Spain it's mandatory to serve tapas with your drinks, so a restaurant down the road from our house became my usual haunt whenever Sean disappeared for a couple of hours. I guzzled down bottle after bottle of wine complemented with plates of sardines, olives, selections of cheese, slices of jamón and entire loaves of bread.

I'd pretty much doubled my weight by the time I finally had the courage to leave him and I guess for most people that would be a normal weight, but right now it's more than I've ever weighed.

"You look *stunning*, babe. Healthy," Peyton says as Harley glowers at her. She's emphasized the word 'healthy' and I don't like it. I know what she really means. I feel it. My legs seem to have doubled in size as if overnight, I can feel them wobble whenever I moved. Cellulite has shown up out of nowhere.

My bodies changing and to me, it's horrifying.

Peyton asks me if I've heard from Sean yet. She's the first person brave enough to mention his name since I'd come home. I hate the way his name sounds at all, let alone on her tongue. I tell her I had heard from him, numerous times now. He's sent me a handful of casual texts asking how I am and when I hadn't responded he started sending me photographs of the beach we used to walk down to every morning at 5am with our coffees.

It's weird seeing images of the place I'd called home for so long, the place I will never go back to.

I've ignored all of his texts, hoping that he'll soon get the message that I don't want to talk to him. He hasn't.

"You're going to find someone so much better than him, I promise you," Kate, another friend of ours, tells me with a pitying look. I want to wipe it off of her face. I can't even fathom being with someone else right now. In my mind, Sean had been the person I was going to spend the rest of my life with before things went south. I was going to finally catch up to my friends, who are already getting married and popping out babies. For the longest time I've been uncertain whether I wanted that myself but a part of me can't help feel left behind. When Sean had come into my life he became my hope... and what's that quote from one of my favorite books, The Girl in 6E by A.R. Torre?

'Hope is dangerous. Hope can be the loose thread that pulls apart your sanity.'

It just doesn't feel like anyone around me really understands what it's like to lose that. It seems like everyone expects me to be sad for a few days and then just dust myself off and move on again, but it isn't that simple. I can't even toy with the idea of starting from scratch all over again. First dates, learning someone else's body, retelling the same stories from my life all over again to someone new. Just thinking about it tires me out.

"She doesn't need a man! She just needs a good shag," Peyton laughs, picking up on the shift in my mood. We all laugh along with her but deep down, I'm sobbing. I want to run and hide, wait until everyone has left the party.

"Best way to get over someone is to get under someone else," Kate teases. I have to admit that sex would be good, but even that's something concerning me.

I don't know how to tell them that no one can ever measure up to the sex life I'd had with Sean. He'd been the first guy to ever make me feel entirely comfortable with my body, stretch-marks and all. It isn't just that though. We did things that I had never done in the bedroom before, things that I could never possibly *imagine* asking someone else to do with me. The way he'd treated me, taking me even when I said no to him, even when I hadn't wanted it. It wasn't consensual but it wasn't rape either. It was a strange thing. Hurting me, slapping my flesh with an aggression that both frightened me and excited me. The way he'd tell me I liked it. It was never a question when he hissed, '*You like that, don't you?*' It was a command. I *would* like it. I *would* endure it… because he liked it.

The thrill of it was intoxicating. I'd hated my body for so long that it felt like a relief to be so open to spreading my legs for someone, because he was never really looking at me. He was looking at what he could do to me. There's a difference. It will never be the same and to be honest, sex is the thing I think I'm going to miss the most about him. Rough sex, they call it. Who would have thought that would be my thing?

I'm swept away by another friend then, who coaxes a glass of wine into my hands. I'm grateful for it and sip a little too quickly as I listen to the latest events of her life. It's a welcomed distraction although I can feel eyes on me from every corner of the room. When Peyton taps the side of her glass with a silver spoon, I flood with heat. I know what's coming. She stands on a palette in the center of the room, hushing everyone while she wows us all with her sparkling white teeth. Her lips are painted plum.

"Right, so this is just going to be a quick speech-" she begins and a couple of our friends muffle their laughter. With Peyton, it's never quick. She adores being in the limelight.

"I think I can say for absolutely all of us that we're happy to have you home, Regan."

Claps and even a couple of cheers follow. I have to admit, it makes me feel good. I squeeze my glass of wine with my clammy hands, fighting back a smile. It's a losing battle.

"It's been a sad few years without the person who always organizes sushi lunches and ladies nights away from the men. You've always been the person we can talk to about anything and the one who takes the best photographs for us." I'm reminded that I'm always the listener, the organized one; always the person behind the camera... never the person in front of it.

While Peyton continues, Harley grabs my hand. I look down at her, trying to remember the times I'd held her hand while we crossed the streets in her younger years. This feels different. I want to squirm away but I can't hurt her feelings, so I leave my hand limply in hers until the speech comes to an end.

"Come and see my room," Harley says, tugging on my sleeve as Peyton comes up to us with her loping gait.

"Yes! You can show her your little sister's room, afterwards," Peyton suggests, offering her daughter a rub on the shoulder.

Harley shrugs away from her, rolling her eyes.

"Come on," she sighs, snaking her arm through mine as we nose our way towards the staircase. Peyton mouths an apology as I twist my head over my shoulder to her.

In my limited experience, teenagers usually don't want adults anywhere near their rooms so Harley dragging me up to hers makes me feel suddenly queasy.

"Harley, I–" I begin as the door to her room shuts behind us.

Her little chest heaves up and down as her breathing quickens. I feel trapped, claustrophobic behind the four walls of her bedroom.

I look around. A messy bookshelf stands in the corner, home to a stack of books with their spines still perfectly intact. Her bed is rumpled, unmade, a ludicrous looking A-cup bra poking out from between the sheets. One of her dresses is strewn carelessly across the floor.

She has one of those dressing tables I'd always wanted as a kid, myself. Makeup litters the surface, tubes of sticky lipstick and bottles of foundation. Her smeared mirror has magazine cutouts stuck all over it.

I look back at her awkwardly; she's still staring at me. It's then I notice her cheeks, brushed with a ghastly amount of red blush that looks ridiculous against her dark skin tone. Her thick lips are slicked with gloss; she hasn't quite grown into her mouth yet. She isn't smiling. It looks as though she wants to say something so I keep quiet, waiting. She's my godchild, I have to act normal yet I feel the furthest from it.

Just as I draw in a breath of sweetened air from her girly deodorant, Peyton barges into the room.

"You can't hog Regan all day, sweetie! Come, I want to show you the nursery," Peyton, completely oblivious to the weird friction between us, leads me away from Harley's room and back across the landing.

"Sorry about her. She's been acting up a bit since the pregnancy..." Peyton whispers, just out of earshot from Harley who is following along behind us. Peyton opens a door to a hideously pink room containing a wooden cot and a rocking chair. Harley snarls as I tell them it's beautiful, or maybe I imagined that.

*

Just over a week later, after my meeting with Peyton in the coffee shop, I receive the call.

"Miss. Regan Pen?"

"Yes, who's speaking?" I ask, there's a crackle on the other end of the line.

"I'm sorry to have to tell you this, but your friend, Peyton Pretorius, was murdered last night.

3

Peyton was stabbed in the stomach forty eight times, killing both her and her unborn child. No weapon was found on the scene. In fact, the cleaning of all forensic evidence seemed to have been meticulous. Whoever the murderer was, they had left absolutely no trace.

Peyton had bled out on the tiles of her kitchen floor.

Harley had found her, the police tell me. She'd knelt down and tried to stop the bleeding although it was already too late, she had coated her hands with her mother's sticky, black blood until she was soaked. Forensics believe that the disembowelment and severing of her fingers happened after death. Neighbors had heard Harley's guttural cries and called the police immediately.

They'd found her sitting catatonically in a pool of blood and amniotic fluid, holding her mother's lifeless body in her lap. Each of Peyton's hacked off fingers had been placed in a wide spread circle to point directly at her body. I try to imagine it, but I can't. This isn't happening. It's too much for me to comprehend.

The police still haven't caught the murderer. There seems to be no possible motive; everyone loves... 'loved' Peyton. So far, they don't even have a lead although they are attempting to locate Peyton's ex for questioning. Their relationship ended badly. It turned out that throughout their time together, he had a wife and child on the side so when she fell pregnant, she denied him any part in her or their baby's lives. There's no evidence to pertain him to the murder so far, though. The detective assures me that they're confident in solving the case and while I wish I could believe them, I don't. Although they're all seasoned investigators, Peyton lived in an area commonly known for violence and rape in the township. There are already hundreds of unsolved cases from the area this year alone. A neighbor reported seeing a grey Nissan X-Trail parked outside of Peyton's house the morning of her murder. The police say they're busy compiling a list of all of the cars of that make and model registered in the town. God knows how long that will take them. They're as fastidious as can be though, conducting interviews with surrounding houses and all of Peyton's closest friends. They've even opened up old case files, looking into people who could be considered for something so horrific. It's only a small town, after all. It's a mammoth sized job nonetheless, but as much as they're trying nothing quite fits the profile yet. They even bring me in to ask some questions. When they ask where I was the night of the murder, it astounds me so much that I laugh. They don't like that.

"I'm sorry; it just sounds like you're accusing me of having something to do with this?" I rap my fingernails on the table, a nervous habit. The detective watches my hands carefully.

"At this stage we aren't ruling anything out, ma'am. As we are no closer to identifying the killer we need to keep all options open."

"That's absolutely ridiculous. I'm her best friend!?" I don't understand why my heart is beating so fast.

"With most cases like this, it very often turns out to be someone close to the victim."

"*Victims...*" I correct cockily.

"We are aware of your stewardess profession, Miss. Pen. Due to the lengths the murderer went to in order to leave no DNA or evidence behind, we need to ask you these questions. Whoever is responsible seems to have quite a knack for cleanliness."

"So you think because I scrubbed some Russian assholes excrement out of toilets for a few years, I'm a suspect?!"

"As I said, we are just trying to do our jobs."

The detective doesn't press too much more out of me after this. He confirms my 'whereabouts' with my landlord, even though I hadn't seen or heard anything from her that night at all.

It takes some time for me to be able to see Harley but soon enough Peyton's will is produced and I'm told that I am legally responsible for the her well-being from now on. Bile rises in my throat and I run into the squalid public bathroom where I keel over a yellow stained toilet seat. I wait for the nausea to subside, which takes some time in a room that reeks of urine, and then return to a room filled with uniformed officers and lawyers. There's a thin film of grease-like sweat shining from my forehead.

I want to tell them that this is a mistake. I can barely look after myself, let alone a teenage girl.

Nothing feels real as Harley's brought into the room. She's swathed in clothing far too big for her, which she clings to tightly. Her eyes are vacant; she doesn't even acknowledge my presence in the room.

"She's in a huge state of shock," a woman I haven't been introduced to tells me. I want to ask questions, but I don't know where to start. Instead I nod dumbly, looking between Harley and the woman across from me.

"She doesn't seem to be able to remember much," the woman continues. She has a name badge clipped to her sumptuous blazer but the letters all seem to mesh together in front of me. I can't concentrate long enough to spell them out. Another woman had taken me aside before entering the room and gravely told me that Harley would need to be placed on suicide watch. I don't even know what all of that entails but I'd pretended to understand everything she'd said to me. Inside, my blood was curdling.

Looking at Harley now, it's easy to see why they've placed her on suicide watch. She still has crusty, coagulated blood beneath her fingernails. It can't be Peyton's. I refuse to believe that she's dead; the most alive person in the world, dead. I'm shell-shocked, trying desperately to keep my composure as I look at her. My heart rips open seeing how empty her eyes are as they bleed into the wall. I have to remind myself that she's just lost her mother, her only blood-relative left. I watch as she gnaws at her jagged nails, wondering if she can taste a metallic tang on her tongue. She licks her lips; it makes me want to vomit again. Her mouth twitches as she looks up at me now, offering me an eerie half smile that none of the police notice. I convulse, swallowing hard, unable to shake the feeling of fear that has worked its way into my bones.

I prolong what the police call 'standard procedures' for as long as I can. I want to stave off her arrival to my home; now *our* home. It makes me feel guilty; I'm disgusted with myself and my selfishness. I haven't had the time to prepare the spare room for her. The room I'd envisioned as my writing room, somewhere to finally hammer out that novel I've been talking about for years. All of my plans suddenly disintegrate around me.

Returning to South Africa was supposed to be my time to finally focus on me. Start over in life, reassemble myself. I was going to be selfish instead of always putting everyone else first. I was planning on finding a new career, becoming whoever I wanted to be. Yet once again someone else has come along and I have to think about them too. For once, it isn't a man. This time, it's my best friend's daughter… and Peyton would probably hate me if she knew how I was feeling right now.

The cottage I'd been so proud of only a few days earlier is suddenly inadequate. It isn't big enough for both of us. We're going to be living on top of one another. What I'd felt to be so comfortable and spacious before now seems like a shoebox. I feel insulted as Harley drags her feet inside; just the way she looks at the place belittles it. "Are you hungry?" I ask her, my words hollow. I feel foolish. I have no idea how to be a parent.

She nods, so I throw together a pasta dish at her behest. I chuck slices of ham I'd thought would last me at least two weeks into a pot and scoop pesto out of a jar which is almost finished after cooking just this one dish. My fridge is a supply for one, not more. I'll need to go shopping again, I realize.

While she unpacks a small bag of her belongings she'd been able to collect from her house, I allow a large sip of wine to slide down my gullet. I need it. My face distorts as tears stream down my cheeks in the moment of privacy. Peyton. My best friend. What has been feeling so surreal now hits me hard and fast. She's gone.

There's a framed photograph of us above the mantle-piece, arms slung around each other. After three more gulps of wine, I stash the bottle in the back of the cupboard and take the photo down. I'm worried that if Harley sees it, it would be too much for her. It's almost too much for me as I grab the frame with shaking hands. I put it in my bathroom, hoping this will be the one place that will still be only mine. I touch her face behind the glass as I place it up on the windowsill.

"I miss you, P," I whisper, then pull myself together splashing cold water onto my face.

By the time we squeeze around my little table to eat, the wine has helped drift me away from reality. It feels good until my mind starts playing tricks on me. Harley looks so much like her mother; it's hard to look at her. The only difference is that Harley has straightened her hair, it looks odd and unnatural.

While Harley wolfs her food down, I twirl the spaghetti around my fork absentmindedly. I can't eat. I don't understand how she can be hungry after what she's just been through. We don't speak. Harley hasn't spoken a word since she's been with me; her responses are all grunts if not nods and shakes of her head. The energy between us is volatile.

After she polishes off two plates of food she scrapes her chair back. It makes me wince, the sound of nails drawing down a chalkboard. She wonders off to my spare room, *her* room, and shuts the door behind her.

It frustrates me how quickly she's made herself at home here. I shove my plate of untouched food into the microwave for safe keeping then pick up her discarded plate to wash it in the sink. I've always found cleaning to be therapeutic and it isn't long before I sublimely loose myself in the sudsy water. Bubbles of washing up liquid float all around me.

The next morning I slink into the kitchen after applying for a handful of new job advertisements. I'm being quieter than I would usually be, afraid to wake her up. I keep myself busy, pottering around with bare feet. I brew some coffee, fighting the urge to uncork the bottle of wine from last night. I look at the clock. It isn't even nine in the morning. *Wait until a reasonable hour*, I tell myself, knowing it's wrong. It scares me that I'm finding myself relying on the one thing that has already destroyed my mother. I just don't know how else to cope right now. On top of dealing with Peyton and Harley, my heart is still broken from Sean and the move back to South Africa has stressed me out more than I'd anticipated. Instead of reaching for the bottle, I push it further back into the depths of the cupboard and grab a pack of pancake mix. I stir together the ingredients, finding solace in food; wanting to make sure Harley doesn't stop eating the way I had done when I was hurting.

When she finally emerges, her hair is returning to its chaotic spirals. There are dark rings beneath her eyes, as though she hasn't slept at all. I hadn't slept well either. My thoughts couldn't be tamed. Images of Peyton's body in a room splattered floor to ceiling with blood had kept me awake. In my mind it looked like something straight out of Dexter.

My stomach growls at me aggressively but I still can't bring myself to touch my food.

"Hungry?" I ask her tentatively, plastering what I hope to be a cheerful look on my face. Asking her if she's hungry has been the only thing I've said to her since she's arrived.

I'm desperate to be her friend, to show her that I'm here for her, but I don't know how. If I'm being honest, I've never been good with her and I never really understood why Peyton had made the outlandish decision to make me her Godmother. She had so many other friends who could have done a better job than me. Where are they now? Reaching out to them seems impossible to me. I don't want them to know I can't handle this.

I'm positive Harley has an acute awareness of my nerves.

She sits at the table and stabs a pancake with her fork. I sit down across from her, wondering if I should ask her about school. It's a Wednesday, but I'm sure she needs some time off right now; at least until after the funeral.

"What do you want to do today?" I ask her eventually.

"Don't you have a job?" Her voice is clipped.

Something about the way she says it makes me feel useless. I feel the hours I've spent pouring my energy into job hunting slip away.

"I just got back, Harley. I'm still looking for one," I say pathetically, laughing at my banality.

She looks at me askew as she crams her mouth full of pancake, syrup dripping onto her chin. She wipes it away with her sleeve. I sigh, knowing I'm going to have to wash it for her later.

"I'm going for a walk," she says, once again leaving her dirty dishes at the table. Rubbing my temple, I tell myself to give her a few days before telling her she needs to do more things around the house. One thing I will not become is her slave.

She slams the front door on her way out and it only occurs to me then that I haven't even taken note of what she's wearing. Isn't that what mothers are supposed to do, in case something happens to her? I'm so out of my element. I peep out of the window, trying to catch sight of her but she is already disappearing down the road. Tears prick at my eyes as I let the curtains fall back in front of me. I don't know if I'm crying because of Peyton's death or because of how small and uncertain I suddenly feel.

Once again I make my way to the sink to wash up after her, feeling like I'm getting stuck in some sort of perpetual motion.

For the rest of the morning I trawl the internet in search of a job. I'm supposed to have been taking more time to find something fitting for me, but now with the pressure of feeding two mouths instead of one, I need to hurry up. My money from the yachts isn't going to last forever. I also feel the need to impress Harley; to be resourceful.

I soon find an advertisement for something in marketing which I apply for instantly. I spend over an hour working on my cover letter, outlining all of the qualities I possess that they're looking for. I make it clear to them in my email that I would be an asset to their team.

Something about this job feels right. Only a few minutes pass by before my phone rings and the company asks if I'm available to come in today for an interview. I'm flummoxed, but jump at the chance and quickly race through the shower. I hope the interviewer won't notice my swollen eyes. No amount of concealer can hide the fact that I've been crying again. I also don't have much in the way of business attire, so I hope my one mint green collared shirt and an outdated black pencil skirt will suffice.

I'm on my way out the door when I realize Harley hasn't returned home yet. I try to call her but it goes straight to voicemail. I don't have the motherly instincts in me to be nervous yet, so instead I fire a message to her to let her know that I'm leaving the key to the house under a plant pot.

I'm driving down the street when I see her, hunched over on the side of the road. She's in such a pitiful state, sobbing into her knees. I pull over and dash towards to her.

"Harley?" I touch the back of her neck, hot and sweaty from the sun beating down onto her. She recoils from me.

"Tell me what I can do?" I ask her helplessly, priming myself for more of her insults.

When finally she lifts her head, she looks up at me with fierce eyes and I am once again startled by the striking resemblance she has to Peyton.

She looks so angry and alone, I desperately want to pull her into my arms and hug her but I'm too scared to touch her again. The sympathy I did possess for her is counteracted with an underlying fear of her that I can't shake.

My mind is close to exploding as ideas of how I can cheer her up fly through my head, each as pointless as the next. There is nothing that can fix things in this moment.

My skirt strains as I crouch beside her, blood pooling at the tips of my toes in my high-heeled shoes. I pull at the sleeves of my shirt which hides the fading bruises on my arms from Sean. The material isn't thick enough to keep me warm from the chilly breeze that blows by despite the cloudless day.

"We can't sit here all day, come on. Let's go take a walk on the beach or something," I suggest as cars whizz by, some of the drivers hooting at me as my car is pulled up illegally on the side of the road. In the car, Harley becomes silent once her sobbing peters out.

"Do you want to talk about her?" I ask. She knows who I mean. Her elbow rests against the open window and she looks out at the ocean on the horizon. She ignores me.

"For fuck sake, Harley! Speak to me!" I slam my hand down onto the steering wheel, my temper getting the better of me. I regret it instantly, but she doesn't even bat an eyelid. Her silence unnerves me. As soon as I pull into the parking lot by the beach, she unbuckles her seatbelt and bolts from the car.

I dig around in my handbag for my phone, needing to hear my dad's voice. He answers on the first ring.

"I don't know what to do, dad. She won't say anything to me!" I tell him, watching Harley's silhouette in the distance. We are at the same beach where I'd met her and Peyton all those years ago. Perhaps I shouldn't have brought her here yet. The thought only occurs to me now.

"She's grieving, darling. You need to be patient with her."

I know he's right. He tells me to go down to the beach and just *be* with her. First, I walk through the market where women are selling handmade wooden bowls and other sorts of African souvenirs. I pass an array of colorful sarongs and floppy hats, looking around. I pick out a little shell bracelet that has just been strung together and two ice creams from a little girl with no front teeth before following Harley's footprints in the sand.

She's up on a dune, so I work my way unsteadily to her, feeling a burn in my gluteal muscles that I haven't felt for ages. I hate the feeling of the dry, grainy sand between my toes.

As I reach her one of the ice creams is plucked from my hand without a thank you. I bite my lip, producing the bracelet and slip it onto her delicate wrist. She looks at me then, curiously.

"I just want you to know that I'm here for you, whenever you're ready," I say, looking out at the waves. She sucks in the salty air.

"I don't know what you want me to say," her voice is hoarse.

We sit in silence for a while, both exhausted until we fall asleep right there in the sand to the sound of the ocean.

◊

I'm not sure how many hours go by before I wake up, looking blearily around me. It takes me a moment to remember why I'm here, with Harley sleeping soundlessly next to me. At some stage she must have put her hand in mine. The bracelet I'd gotten her has pressed itself into my arm, leaving small indentations in my skin. I drop her hand into the sand, freaked out by how intimate we must have looked while we slept.

"Oh, no!" I cry, scrambling to my feet as it dawns on me that I've missed my interview. Harley shoots up, her coarse hair awry from sleep.

"What?!" she gasps, immediately on edge.

"I missed my interview," I sigh, squeezing my eyes together, ruining the makeup I'd applied earlier. I'm gutted and Harley can see it. She smirks.

"This isn't funny, Harley," I say irritably, already storming back towards the car.

"Regan," she booms, her voice is so commanding that I stop in my tracks and slowly turn around to face her. She appears hurt and looks so small in comparison to our surroundings.

I wait for her to speak again, and when she does she has an ominous smile painted her face.

"I thought you wanted to spend time with me?"

4

Bodies look nothing like the serene, peaceful corpses you see in the movies. Peyton chose to have an open casket, and as I look down at her it isn't really her at all. She is just a body. Lifeless. It doesn't even look like her anymore without blood running through her veins and air in her lungs.

I'm thankful that the toy-like casket chosen for her eight month fetus is closed, at least. It's hard to imagine the mutilation that must have been done to the body while still inside Peyton's womb. Her name was going to be Nova, she'd told me that once or twice before but it became all the more real as I see her name printed on the obituary.

Two caskets stand on show with one large photograph balancing on an easel between them; an image of an apple-cheeked Peyton, glowing with her pregnancy as she holds proudly onto her stomach. The room is pungent with the overpowering scent of lilies and swarming with people dressed in black. These people are my friends. They had all been at my reunion, but I can't look at any of them now. None of them would have been my friend if it weren't for Peyton anyway.

It's a relief to be out in the cemetery after the service. As the hearse draws away on the gravel road I watch Harley throw a handful of daisies over her mother's open grave.

"And by throwing flowers into the earth, so flowers shall grow again," the priest says glibly. The whole mundane affair is like nothing I would have chosen for Peyton, personally. I'd have gone for cremation; the thought of her hair and nails continuing to grow under the ground freaks me out too much.

It feels strange to be having the funeral when we're still no steps closer to determining who the murderer is. There's no closure. Peyton's ex has been vindicated from her death and he's here today, paying his respects. Gallant or not, I still despise him for the way he treated her. He stays longer beside Nova's casket, his unborn daughter; his tears raw and real. No part of me feels any sympathy for him.

In my swirling bitterness I realize I'm starting to develop pretty hateful feelings towards all men in general. It sounds stupid, but for once I want to be the user and abuser. I have this visceral fear that I'll never be able to love someone again and that's why I wind up at a local pub shortly after the funeral comes to an end. I want to fuck it all away with a one night stand.

Luckily, Harley's chosen to be with a team of her dense friends and I cherish the stolen time away from her. As each day with her passes, the tension between us grows. I've become well aware of her rifling through my drawers when I'm out; sifting through my makeup and clothes. Things aren't where I left them, they never are anymore. I feel violated by the intrusion. Sometimes I notice her nails painted in my shade of red or I see that she's wound one of my scarves around her neck. Even as things have started to go missing entirely, bottles of my perfume that I can smell on her and tubes of my expensive lipstick I know she's taken, I choose to ignore it. I know I'm being too lenient with her but I just want us to get through this funeral. I hope that the mechanics of our relationship will get better after this.

I have on a little black dress that ties together at the back with a frivolous ribbon. It digs into my spine as I lean back on the bar stool. The man behind the bar offers me a shot of tequila and I welcome it graciously, sucking greedily onto a lemon.

There are a couple of men glancing my way inside of the pub, even with my indistinct features. My mousy brown hair is braided and my grey-blue eyes accentuated with pricey makeup. I've put some bronzer on to mask my pale skin and a shimmering body lotion that smells of coconut. Dressing up makes me feel a little bit better and that's what I need right now. Call me a narcissist. My best friend's just been murdered and all I care about is looking sexy enough to find a shag for the evening.

Women showing even a little bit of skin in my tiny town are sure to receive attention. It won't be hard to find someone to help me take the pain away, if only momentarily. I just need to have sex. I can't stand the fact that the last person to be inside of me is Sean. I want him gone from me and my body.

I ignore the barman's unsubtle attempts of flirting with me, locking my eyes on a robust looking man with peppered grey hair who hasn't shot me any looks so far. He's been too busy concentrating on his phone. I suddenly feel up for a challenge.

He is affable enough as we polish off a bottle of whiskey under the watchful eye of the barman. My puffy eyes are excused after I tell him I've just come from my best friend's funeral, and he gives me a sympathy fuck in the dingy bathroom. I'm bent over, doggy-style, gripping the sides of the porcelain toilet as he slackens his belt and rams into me. Grabbing fistfuls of my hair, my head is thrust back to lean into him and I love it. It feels angry and carnal. He muffles my cries with the palm of his hand and breathes drunkenly into my neck as he pulls out of me, squirting all over my bare back. We haven't used protection but in this moment, I don't care. All I can smell is alcohol and sex as we rearrange ourselves. My tights ladder as I pull them roughly up my legs, making us both laugh. He tells me his name is Jamie and puts his number into my phone, but I know I'll never use it.

He leaves shortly after that, leaving me alone with our bar tab. I should have known, but I'm so drunk that I don't mind that he's used me. I sit back down at my seat, feeling raw in between my legs. I order another tumbler of whiskey.

"I'd really appreciate it if you didn't have sex in my bar," the barman tells me outright. I laugh, feeling no shame. The way he looks at me annoys me.

I don't have enough money in my purse to pay for the bottle of whiskey so the barman offers me a ride home so I can get some cash from inside. It's well past closing hour, anyway.

I stagger to his car, a rusted hatchback that holds a strong aroma of air-freshener inside. He tries making small talk with me along the drive to the cottage but the slow movements of his driving soon lulls me to sleep. When he pats me awake his face is unfamiliar for a few seconds; the hangover already taking hold. My chin is wet with drool. I groan and stretch in the cramped space I've found myself in. I open the car door and topple out onto the ground. He chuckles but when I turn around to glare at him, he looks down at me innocuously.

After helping me up he walks me to the porch.

"Wait here," I say, putting my hand to his chest to stop him from coming inside with me. For a fleeting moment my vision tunnels and I find myself stroking the buttons of his shirt. He smiles at me, taking me by the shoulders and twirling me away from him.

"I wouldn't come inside even if you did invite me in," he says. I'm not sure if this should offend me or not. I unlock my front door and leave him outside while I go scratch around for some money.

As I'm diving in and out of numerous handbags, retrieving as many scrunched up notes and loose coins as I can, I hear voices coming from the porch. Wondering who he could be talking to I pause and crane my neck around the wall to listen. There's a ringing in my ears making it impossible for me to hear anything. I catch sight of myself in the mirror. My hair's a matted mess, sticking out at all sorts of angles. My mascara's smudged down the side of my face I'd been sleeping on in his car. My lipstick's rubbed off and my lips are dried and chapped, stained with patches of red wine from earlier in the evening. I'm pale and my eyes can't focus properly as I try to coil my hair up into a messy bun. It's a failed attempt at fixing my disgusting appearance.

Trying to walk in a straight line, I somehow manage to make my way back to the front door without knocking anything over. My landlord stands on the porch alongside my barman. I instantly sober up, or at least I think I do.

"Hello!" I say, overfriendly.

"Oh – Regan, have you seen Jasper?"

"Sorry. Have I seen *who*?" I'm confused. I've never heard that name before in my life.

"Jasper, my cat," she looks crestfallen as I shake my head. It makes me dizzy.

I assure her that I'll call her if I see her cat. She ambles away after giving the barman an austere look. Once she's wandered back to her house down the way I hand him a wad of cash that I hope will be sufficient payment.

"Thanks..." I say awkwardly, only just realizing I don't even know his name. He must read my mind.

"Craig," he laughs, tucking the money into the pocket of his jeans.

"Right, Craig. I'm Regan."

"I know," he grins, starting back towards his car. I watch him go, marveling at his ass while holding myself up with the doorframe. He turns back and catches me staring. I plunge inside of the cottage, mortified.

"I'll see you around, Regan!" he calls before climbing into his car.

I'm high on booze and sex as I lock the door behind me, not yet ready to go to bed. Instead, I keep myself busy with collecting enough laundry to put on to wash.

I swig from the bottle wine hidden in the cupboard behind a stack of soup tins I feel too bad to give to Harley as dinner. I'm almost certain there had been more in the bottle when I'd put it there. My eyes catch sight of the picture of Peyton and me. I smile at it sadly. I desperately want to hear her voice again; hug her, smell her. It feels strange to be carrying on without her. Harley and I have started seeing a counselor and although it feels good to be able to speak about Peyton to someone, I do feel like it's a bit of a waste of money. The price for one session is astronomical and Harley apparently lets the hours tick by without saying a word. I on the other hand have a lot to say. I can't speak about Peyton to Harley and I feel the need to keep her spirit alive, afraid if I stop speaking about her I'll forget her and her little intricacies that made her who she was. I've spoken to the therapist about Sean, too. It dawned on me the other day that I don't have anyone else to speak to anymore. I'm too proud to go to my parents and my best friend had been eradicated from my life.

I put the wine bottle beside the frame, leaving a rim of red on the glossy white tiles in my bathroom.

Hesitantly, I push the door open to Harley's room, feeling as though I'm invading her space. It's an absolute tip. As I gather up a heap of her scattered sweaters and dresses, my eyes fall onto a pair of ripped denim jeans. They're covered in cat hair.

◊

I guess the gesture could have been considered sweet when days later after no sign of Jasper, Harley brought home a kitten. My landlord had taken one look at it, all fluff, large olive eyes and whiskers, before bursting into tears. She'd told us that her cat couldn't be replaced and wanted us to take it back to the animal welfare straight away. I wanted the same thing, but Harley's eyes had glistened with tears of her own as she told me she needed the company. She also said if we didn't keep it, it would be gassed and killed because the welfare was overrun with animals needing homes. She'd stared me down with a derisive look. Of course I thought it was a fallacy, but Harley knew just how to squash me under her thumb.

I started to think that maybe a cat would be good for her, hoping it would be the solution to the problems we'd been having since she'd moved in. I caved eventually, splurging money I didn't have on litter boxes, catnip and jingly toys that got under my feet. It had made her full of zeal at first and I thought that I'd finally done something right. I should have known it wouldn't be that easy and infallible though.

She's refused to empty out the litter box, claiming she has a weak stomach. In fact, she's barely looked at the cat since I allowed it to stay and, just like with Harley, if I don't take care of it, no one will.

5

It's a Sunday evening when Harley announces she's ready to go back to school. We're sitting around my rickety table and I've been trying not to watch as she sucks the sinew from the meat I'd prepared for us earlier that day.

"That's great!" I say, overenthusiastically. I'm looking forward to the few hours without her more than I like to admit. Having her constantly in my space, watching me day in and day out, makes me feel like I have to tiptoe around my own home. Carving out some alone time has proven to be more difficult than I'd imagined so I couldn't be more grateful to the school for offering some respite from her.

"I'll need you to take me there in the morning and pick me up afterwards."

I try to hide my irritation at the thought of becoming her personal chaperone.

"Isn't there a bus, or something?" I ask, hopeful. Her gaudy expression falls flat.

"No one takes the bus."

"If that was the case I'm sure there wouldn't *be* a bus," I counter. We stare at each other tediously, neither one of us wanting to back down.

In a town as small as this one, finding another job to apply for is challenging. I've lost my chances at the marketing firm, regardless of the apologetic email I'd typed out hurriedly to them.

All of the money I'd worked so hard for in Europe is dwindling away and the stress is mounting up. My shoulders ache from being hunched over my laptop for hours on end, searching for what I believe to be a non-existent job. I've finally come across something that sounds right up my street; a manager for a small, bohemian café. It's within walking distance from the cottage.

"You're going to have to catch the bus back, Harley. I have a job interview at three," I say the following day as I'm shuttling her to the local high-school. She's hiked her pleated skirt up far too high and there are already stains from what appears to be jam on the white collared shirt she'd asked me to iron.

"I can't take the bus!"

I grip the steering wheel, tight.

"Regan, I said I can't take the bus," she says after I don't reply for a while. I keep staring at the road in front of us, counting to ten in my head.

"Regan?"

When again I don't acknowledge her she starts repeating my name over and over again, almost demonically. It's the kind of behavior I'd expect from a five year old. As her voice escalates, I close my eyes just briefly. I'm exhausted.

"Regan!" she screams and my eyes fly open. The car in front of us has come to an abrupt halt and I hadn't been paying attention. I swerve, almost sending us directly into the oncoming traffic. "Jesus Christ, Harley! Can you just shut up? You're such a fucking distraction," the words escape my mouth before I have a chance to catch them. Her jaw slacks open as she looks at me with disbelief. I try to apologize but she wrenches the car door open and runs straight into the traffic. I don't know how she isn't run over. When eventually she comes home, hours after school has broken; she slams the door to her room and locks it behind her. I'd been too guilt-ridden to go to my interview that afternoon and had spent my day preparing a Shepherd's Pie for our supper. It's left cold and untouched. The only thing I need to wash up is a wine glass. I can't remember the last time I actually ate something. I pop two pain killers to ease my throbbing headache and drift off into a dreamless sleep.

Harley leaves for school the next morning before I've even woken up. I ring the school to make sure she arrived safely before I can relax. With her out of the house again, I take the opportunity to spring clean her room. I'm not sure if she'll be happy with me going through her room but it's filthy and I want to do something to show her how sorry I am. I didn't even know I was looking for something until it's in my hands. I hold the hard-covered, garish journal and wonder if I should open it. I want to get inside her head. I want to get to know her, figure her out. In the end, curiosity wins and the spine cracks as I gingerly open it. Pages upon pages of idiosyncratic, messy cursive are revealed along with what looks like dried blood smeared onto some of the pages. I leaf through the book, flipping to the most recent entry. It's from last night, almost unreadable in its angry scratchiness.

You'd think that now my mum and 'Nova' are gone, things would be getting better but Regan is too busy with her own pathetic life to notice me.

I feel a stab of guilt right in my gut, mixed with offense and confusion. It feels so silly that words written by a thirteen year old girl can hurt me this much. I don't understand the entry at all. Why would things be getting better without her mother? I flip further back in the book to when Peyton was still alive.

I hate that I'm having these thoughts. This is the only place I can let them out, though. I wish she would miscarry, but it's probably too late for that now. I prayed for months that my sister would drop from her cunt but it never happened. Maybe God doesn't exist. My prayers were never answered and now I know I need to take matters into my own hands if I want to stop this from happening. Sometimes I think about pushing her down the stairs, getting rid of it that way... If I got lucky, mum would break her neck in the fall and finally be gone too. I know if I do that I'll never really forgive myself, though. I don't know what to do.

I feel sick to my stomach as I hold her journal in my trembling hands. I'm sure this is the evidence the police need. It isn't a book filled with glitter and lipstick kisses, rambles about her latest crush like a normal thirteen year olds journal should be; like mine had been. This feels like a confession. A key twists in the lock by the front door, fear grasping ahold of me. My breathing quickens as I pull out my phone, taking photographs of the entry as quickly as I can. Hoping I've placed the journal back exactly as it was, I turn around just as Harley rounds the corner and enters her room.

"What are you doing in here?" she demands, standing in the way of the only possible exit. My heart beats so erratically I can feel it all the way down to my feet. My knees wobble and for a moment I'm scared they're going to give way.

"Cleaning," I stutter, my voice hitched too high.

"Get out," she says, still standing in front of the door; trapping me. I walk towards her, my breathing quivering as I stand mere centimeters from her. She takes a step towards me, closing the space between us. Her nostrils flare and her dark eyes glare at me intimidatingly. I don't know how long we stand like this for, but it feels like hours. I'm idling in front of her, too scared to even blink. She is so close that I could count the constellation of freckles scattered on the bridge of her nose. She has little lines branching out from the sides of her eyes, telling stories I wish I knew. When she finally steps aside, I've never felt more inferior or out of control of a situation.

She throws the door shut behind me, making the entire cottage rattle. I hear the key slip into the lock and turn, locking herself away from the outside world. I venture down the echoing hallway, dumbfounded, and do exactly the same thing.

6

The words from Harley's journal roll through my head throughout the night, tormenting me. I'm on high alert every time the cottage creaks, whenever the geyser groans. My eyes twitch from lack of sleep by the time daylight breaks.

The moment she leaves for school on foot, I free myself from the safety of my room. I don't even allow for a shower before locking up and heading towards my car. Autumn leaves coat the driveway, rustling in the wind and crunching beneath my feet. I want to get to the police station, show them the entries from Harley's journal. My car sags closer to the ground than normal, making me look down at the tires. They're all flat. I curse aloud. Harley's cat purrs, blinking up at me in the sunlight as she bathes herself on the bonnet of the car. I look at her disdainfully before starting off down the road on foot. I should have just taken Harley to school this morning. Karma's a bitch, as they say.

◊

"You need to bring us the actual journal and even then, it isn't actually proof that it was her that committed the crime," a bored police officer tells me when I finally arrive at the station.

"But it's right here in black and white. What she was writing in that book isn't normal!" I'm shoving my phone under his nose, but it's getting me nowhere.

"Children write bad things about their parents all the time. Bringing us red herrings such as this is only going to complicate the case further."

I can tell he thinks what I'm showing him is trivial, that I'm wasting his time. He wants me to leave.

"So what happens when I bring you the book and Harley finds out it's missing?"

"Then we'll look into it, ma'am, but as I've already said, we are doing everything possible to solve the case as it is."

I bite my tongue, stopping myself from telling him how useless he is and storm out of the police station, outraged. I need them on my side. I need *someone* on my side.

The walk to the bar is ghastly in the bitter cold. Craig's car is parked outside like I knew it would be, although I wonder how I remember the sort of car he has in the state I'd been in.

"Bit early, don't you think?" he winks at me as I blow inside. I roll my eyes at him.

"I'm not here for a drink," I tell him, though a gin would definitely have taken the edge off right now. He wipes down the counters with a damp cloth, the sleeves of his shirt are rolled up. He has a tattoo I can't decipher snaking up his arm and a loose fitting copper bangle on his wrist. I'm taken-aback by how good looking he is and try to hide the sheer embarrassment I feel for how he'd seen me just days before.

"Then what is it I can do for you, Regan?"

"Can you change a tire, Craig?" I ask, emphasizing his name. I think he's surprised I can remember it. He nods hesitantly.

"Good, because I have four," I say, a small grin spreading across my face as he looks at me ruefully.

I offer him tea or coffee when we get back to the cottage with four new tires crammed into his backseat. He opts for tea and while I make us a pot, he gets to work.

I busy stirring honey into my cup when I look out of the window. I notice he's removed his shirt. His body is deliciously chiseled and the tattoo I'd seen earlier trails all the way up onto his shoulder and chest. I bite my lip. He looks nothing like Sean and that's a good thing.

Sean has dirty blonde hair, always shaggy from salt-water and ocean blue eyes so fitting for the surfer boy look. He has a strong jaw, full lips always curved into a cheeky smile and a bit of a stomach on him; but he is also the kind of guy that knows how attractive he is. It's something he always uses to his advantage. Craig is taller, leaner. His hair is dark with a luster to it, receding at the top and his eyes a peculiar shade of hazel. He has a nose too big for his face which makes him look kind of edgier, but his imperfections make him all the more endearing.

Everything about him is much less striking than Sean initially, but as I stare longer, I realize just how handsome he actually is. He, unlike Sean, has no idea how attractive he is. There's nothing quite as attractive as that.

I don't like that I'm comparing them but I can't help it. I want him. I want him for more than just sex, too, which scares me. I really wasn't expecting to imagine myself with someone else so soon after Sean. I'm in trouble here, and I know it.

As I let the teabags seep, I tear myself away from the view of Craig and walk down to Harley's bedroom. Twisting the door handle I see that she's locked it. I wonder how I'm going to get in there to retrieve the journal. The bucket of keys in the kitchen don't have any that fit the lock. There's only one and Harley has it.

Craig stops for a break in between changing the tires, resting beside me on the porch.

"Who did this to your tires by the way?" he asks me curiously. Sweat glistens on his forehead and upper lip. I don't know if I should tell him. I'm so scared of sounding crazy. I shrug and squint up at the sky.

As a thank you, I make him lunch. Kale, broccoli and chicken chucked into a pan with noodles, ginger, chili and garlic. The kitchen is soon infused with spices and for once I'm happy to have concocted something for another person.

He asks me so many questions about myself that it starts to sound like an interview. He probes minuscule details out of me like who I know here, who my friends are. He slowly drills his way down to the core of me. How my experience was with working on the yachts, why I'd left. I find myself opening up to him about Sean, sharing those nitty-gritty details I haven't spoken to anyone about barring my therapist. He seems genuinely interested in getting to know me and the best part is that I don't have to pay him to speak about myself.

I try to laugh off the fact that Sean had been cheating on me for the duration of our relationship. I want to sound jokey, blasé, but I can tell that he can see right through me. When I tell him Sean had started to hit me after I found out he'd been cheating, he sucks in a breath and shakes his head.

"I'm sorry, that makes me so angry," he says, touching my forearm. The squiggly hairs on his fingers are brittle, I want to place my other hand over his but I'm too shy. The feeling of being touched so gently by a man again is so wonderful; I don't want to break the spell.

"How long did you stay with him after he hit you?"

"A while..." I admit, shame washing over me.

"Why?" his voice is strained.

"You'll think it's a stupid reason."

"Probably," he squeezes my arm and smiles at me encouragingly. I try smiling back but it's so hard.

"OK..." I suck in a deep breath and straighten in the chair, keeping my eyes glued on tiny grains of salt that had landed on the table. I don't want to see the look on his face as I tell him everything.

"I felt like it was my fault that he got aggressive. After I found out what he'd done, he said he'd do anything to make it up to me. He said I meant more to him than any of the other girls and that he knew he'd made a mistake. I remember he actually cried when he told me he didn't even know why he'd done it, he just wanted attention. I never really understood that because I thought I gave him more than enough attention, but he seemed so genuine, you know?"

Craig nods quietly, frowning as though it pained him to be listening to this.

"He told me he'd been really badly hurt in the past by this girl called Monica and he said he'd always been so scared to think seriously of me because of that. He said he didn't want to get hurt again. For the whole year we were together I was convinced we were as serious as you could get without putting rings on our fingers. We lived together in a country where I had no family close by and the only friends I had were his. I'd kind of just slotted into his world and made it mine. Any life I'd had before him had literally been obliterated so I had nothing to come back to here in South Africa. Knowing that, I decided I wanted to try and fix us. It was the only life I had, so I had to try. I told him he needed to tell all of the women about me. I watched him send the same message to all of them before blocking them all and deleting their numbers. He told me the thought of losing me made him realize how serious he was about me and he'd cried again when he said he was sorry and that he hoped it wasn't too late. I fell for everything he said," I stop, shaking my head and rubbing my eyes with my fist. I wasn't expecting to get quite as emotional about it.

"Anyway... the 'groveling' lasted for about a day. There was a bouquet of flowers and a meal out at El Aquanauta but after that, he turned right back to his old self. Being really secretive, hiding his phone from me, not answering calls whenever I was around. It really affected me and I started feeling certain he was still cheating. I was so paranoid; it ate away at me like a cancer. The person I was before Sean literally collapsed. We started fighting, a lot. The flowers hadn't even died yet before they were thrown against the wall, smashing the vase and making an absolute mess. That's how it started; then things escalated. He started drinking a lot, telling me it was because he hated that I couldn't trust him anymore. He wanted things to go back to how they had been before. I'd been so different then. I wasn't concerned about anything. I never asked questions or felt insecure. After he cheated, everything changed. One of our friends spoke to me about it and said that if we had any chance of making it work I'd have to let go of what he'd done. They said I couldn't hold onto it and use it as ammunition against him whenever we fought and I realized that I couldn't do it. I started initiating fights, pushing him and reminding him of what he'd done and why things were so shitty between us now. I pushed him over the edge," my voice breaks and to my horror I start to cry. Big, heavy tears that have been a long time coming.

"It got toxic," he says, scooting closer to me and rubbing my shoulders as I try to reassert my composure. I nod, sniffing.

"I'm sorry," I say.

"Don't be! I asked you about it, I want to know all there is to know about you, Regan."

I give him a grateful look, dabbing at my blotchy face with a kitchen towel.

"Come by the pub again later if you're free," he says as I walk him out the cottage. I tell him I might and thank him for his help, wrapping my arms around his neck. His body feels so unfamiliar to me as we hug; so unlike the meatiness of Sean's. I feel equally safe and thrilled in his arms and could stay there for hours. I lose myself in him momentarily but the peacefulness doesn't last long as he pulls away and backs out of the driveway.

I have a few more messages from Sean on my phone when I check it again. There's still no apology, just nonsensical rambles about his day and pictures of him out on the kayak we used to go fishing in together.

One of my girlfriends from the island has already told me that he's seeing one of the girls he cheated on me with. It hurts even more knowing he's with one of those women rather than someone entirely new. I feel replaced and wonder if she knows he's still trying to talk to me, whoever she is.

I can't help but wonder how many women he's talking to behind her back and can't stand that I hate her more than I hate Sean right now. Yet I still feel oddly sorry for her. I'm so fucking confused. Blocking him has been a long time coming and somehow the conversation with Craig about it seems to have given me a courage that hadn't been there before. I finally see that it's not good for me to have him constantly there on my phone as a reminder. Even so, it's still one of the hardest things I've ever had to do.

My finger hovers over the block button for a long moment, thoughts of everything he's done to me racing through my mind; the lying, the cheating, the manipulation. The violence and bruises hit me again so hard that I feel lightheaded.

The insurmountable heartbreak I'd felt the day I'd found out shocked me all over again like a lightning bolt coursing through every nerve in my body. All of that anxiety and stress he caused me both physically and emotionally that had destroyed me resurfaced.

I press down and breathe out a sigh of relief.

It's done.

That chapter of my life is finally over.

I wish Peyton were here to see that I finally did it.

◊

After trying and failing to picklock Harley's bedroom door, I celebrate detaching myself from Sean with bottle of wine and some Tracy Chapman. I know it's too early to be drinking, but I feel liberated. I'd love to be able to see his face when he sees I've actually blocked him. It would be priceless. The thought of it makes me smile with a growing confidence I thought I'd lost forever. Harley's still at school for a few hours so I sit out in a shady spot on the porch and sip happily on the wine. I don't even mind giving the cat a tickle behind her ears when she curls up next to me. It's the first time in weeks I haven't felt so wrung-out. It's like I've finally stopped fighting the current and have started going with the flow, letting it take me where it may.

I scrub my teeth and spray on some perfume before heading to counseling, leaving a note for Harley on the counter about the left over stir-fry. I'll head to Craig's bar right after the session.

I'm excited to see him again. I've got that giddiness you get from a new relationship, even though nothing has technically happened between us yet. The feeling has come on so fast and so strong that I'm practically gushing about it to the therapist, who isn't quite as enthusiastic as me. He tells me I have to be careful about falling for the *idea* of being in a relationship rather than falling for Craig himself. I guess it makes sense. It bursts my bubble and irritates me more than it should.

For the rest of the session the talk centers on Harley. I try prying information from him about his sessions with her but with the patient confidentiality rules I'm having no luck. The best I get from him is when he pushes his wire-framed spectacles up him nose and tells me she's very troubled. That much is already evident and I tell him so. It doesn't take a psychology degree to figure that out. He doesn't appreciate my remarks.

He doesn't even seem too worried about the contents of her diary. Despite the outcome of the meeting, there's still a slight skip in my step as I walk into the bar and lock eyes with Craig. His shirt is back on, much to my disappointment. He still looks good.

"Wine?" he asks me, already taking a glass from the racks hanging above his head. I like how he already knows my preference right down to the grape.

Although the bar fills with people as the working day comes to an end, I can tell I'm Craig's main focus. It makes me feel good. We speaks for hours, watching people come and go; walk in sober and eventually stumble back out. It seems like some sort of hilarious show but it also makes me conscious about the amount I drink. I want to hold my liquor tonight. I have plans involving a pack of condoms, Craig and my bed. Somehow I just know it's going to happen. I've prepared for the event with a wax before leaving the house although regrettably my skin is sticky now despite slapping coconut oil all over the area. I've also got blood blisters and hope to God he won't want the light on so I can hide them. This never happens when I go to an actual beautician. I make a mental note to never do it myself again.

By the time the last straggler pays up, Craig locks the door and joins me by the fading fireplace for one last drink. It's so quiet without the rumble of rowdy people and I notice for the first time just how nervous I am. The setting is so intimate. It's been a long time since I've been alone like this with a man.

Our voices simmer down to whispers as we work our way closer together. When his hand rests on my thigh it shoots heat all the way up to my tingling groin. I lean in and let his other hand cup my chin, pulling me closer until our lips meet. It's so soft and explorative, but at the same time almost cautious as our tongues played gently with one another. I wish the moment never had to end.

We're interrupted by my phone lighting up on the counter. An image of Harley and I appear on the screen as she attempts to call me. It's a picture I haven't seen before. We're on the beach. I'm sleeping in the sand and she's leaning in close to me taking the photograph, showing off her gigantic smile. I find it odd that she'd have that photo up considering how bad our relationship seems right now. I'm also severely freaked out that she's taken a photo of me while I was sleeping. A shudder creeps up my spine and I shiver involuntarily.

"Who's that?" Craig whispers affectionately into my ear. I frown.

"It's no one..."

Instead of feeling guilty, I straddle him, desperate for the moment to come back. His touch is intoxicating as he roams my body, discovering every curve and crevice I have to offer.

"I thought you said no sex in your bar," I tease him and he stifles a laugh into my neck.

"You're right. Your place?" he asks. I nod, forgetting all about the thirteen year old girl who is waiting at home for me.

I'm surprised by how good the sex is. I've been so concerned that sex would never be the same with anyone else after Sean, but Craig is even better. It shocks and exhilarates me all at once and I never want it to end as our bodies ebb and flow.

He takes his time, taking care of me first by kissing every inch of my body. His tongue massages my clitoris with such vigor that I can't breathe; I shudder and shake from more orgasms than I can count. His fingers dip in and out of my wetness so skillfully that I can't contain my cries of pleasure as I bite down hard onto his shoulder blade. His clipped nails draw down my bare back and grasp hold of my love handles, squeezing just to the point of pain before letting go again.

I love feeling the size of him in my mouth, listening to his deep moans as I lick the sweet juice from the tip of his dick and hold his balls in my hands.

When he's finally inside of me I throw my legs, slick with sweat, over his shoulders. We connect on a level I have never experienced before... and he's big! Bloody big. I can feel him right up against my wall, filling me completely. It hurts in the best possible way.

It's while we're sprawled out across my bed with the blankets at our feet, catching our breaths with our limbs intertwined when we hear the shower turn on. He looks up at me.

"Is someone here?"

I haven't told him about Harley and to be honest I'd momentarily forgotten all about her.

I'm suddenly very aware of how loud we were and for a split second I wonder if I'd done it on purpose in some attempt to gain back my dominance.

"It's my Godchild, she moved in with me after Peyton..." my voice trails off. I can't bring myself to say that she's been murdered, not again.

Craig holds me tightly and kisses the top of my head. We listen to the flow of the water in silence as he strokes my arms with his calloused fingertips.

I don't think either of us notice when the shower turns off. I'm too busy planting kisses down his stomach. He's holding tightly onto my hair, pushing me down onto his cock when the door opens. We both startle and I fly up from between his legs. He springs free from my mouth and I grab the blankets to cover us both as Harley switches on my bedroom light. She gapes at us from the doorway, in nothing more than a towel that drops to the floor from shock. She makes no effort to hide her youthful, budding breasts that wobble slightly as she backs away from us. Her hip bones jut out to a nauseating degree. A look of horror spreads across her face. Her body is so tiny and tight, hairless. Craig shields his eyes as Harley lets out a high-pitched squeal. It doesn't sound real.

Her hair is wet, droplets of water hardening her dark nipples. I don't want to look but at the same time I can't look away.

She's caked on a mass amount of ostentatious makeup. I know then and there that she's done this deliberately. She continues to back away, smirking at me while Craig's eyes are still tightly shut.

7

Craig promises me that everything is OK, but as he redresses and hurries out of the cottage I know it's not. I wish I hadn't been so elusive about Harley in the beginning, but it had been nice to pretend I had my old life back for a while. I don't want to be the girl in her late twenties with a harrowing amount of responsibilities; unemployed, major commitment and trust issues after what Sean did to me, drinking problems, crazy mother and trying to look after a deranged teenager. I sound like that girl from Shameless. If running away were an option, I'd do it.

"What the hell was that?!" I scream once he's driven away. I bang on her bedroom door with my fist. I'm so enraged that I don't care if the landlord can hear me or not. I'm not sure if Harley did that to entice Craig or to drive him away. Right now it feels like a bit of both.

I'm not expecting her to open up the door, so when she does I'm pleased to see she's put some clothing on.

"Harley, you dare pull a move like that again and I swear to fucking God you're out on your ass," my voice is still an octave too high.

"Boy, you sure know how to use that mouth of yours don't you?"

she responds drily. Her eyes are lurid, full with an audacity that terrifies me. I narrow my eyes at her, having no clue how to respond. I'm beyond embarrassed that she's caught me going down on Craig and hate that it's me feeling like the teenager right now instead of her. I choose to ignore her comment. I'm exhausted from her antagonizing me and need to get away from her.

"We're having dinner at my parent's tomorrow night. Wear something *appropriate*," I look her up and down.

As I was walking away I hear her say, "Oh, I'll be sure to put *something* on."

◊

The best way to describe what Harley decides to wear to dinner with my parents would be a 'frock.' It's nothing I've ever seen her in before and I wonder where she got it from. It's far from her usual guise, making her look ridiculously young and innocent. It wins my folks over in seconds, but then they are easily duped.

"We're so happy to have you here!" my mother gushes benevolently as Harley gets wrapped into her embrace. I can tell she's been drinking already but what shocks me most is that she's practically the same size as Harley. The booze has shriveled her so much that her body is now that of a teenage girl. How come the more I drink the more weight I put on yet with her it's the opposite? I've already bid the gap between my thighs goodbye.

My mum has on an apricot colored poncho that clashes drastically with her frizzy red hair. I wonder when last she looked in a mirror. I walk right past her before she has the chance to hug me too, heading straight to the bar. It's the first thing anyone does when they visit my parents place. They'd made drinking a mandatory thing. The entire house reeks of dog. It's a damp, potent smell that gets under your nose and stays there. I barely notice it anymore.

I hug my dad hello, knowing my mother is looking and knowing it hurts her that I'm affectionate to him but not her. I don't like being so cruel to her, but I do it anyway. It's my way of showing her that she needs to change. I won't forgive her until she does.

Dad pours me a glass of Shiraz; I've needed it all day.

We speak for a while. I enjoy the formalities of catching up with him in the smoke-filled bar area. I've never thought I'd end up having a close relationship with him, but now he's the person I'm closest to in my family. I guess it has grown overtime as I've gotten older, once my resentment towards him had simmered down. I used to hate him. He has his own history with alcoholism and aggression which had made it impossible for us to connect when I was younger. I still believe his influence is what triggered my mother to develop as big of an addiction as she has today.

"How're things going with Harley?" he asks, pulling on his cigarette. The way he says her name irritated me. He'd already besotted with her.

My dad has this natural affinity towards anything broken. He's a big softie at heart, especially when it comes to children.

"Worse," I mumble, slumping over the counter, retreating back to my adolescent demeanor. Mum and Harley are nattering away in the background.

"You need to start getting used to having her around, Regan."

"She's not normal, dad!" I protest. He looks at me sternly. I don't know how to articulate how uncomfortable she makes me, there seems to be excuses for everything she does.

"She's just lost her mother, Regan. You need to be more understanding. Your problem is that you've never had this kind of responsibility before."

My irritation rises; he knows nothing about the kind of responsibility I've had to deal with lately and the things I've had to endure over recent years. He has no idea what I've been through, not really.

I look over to where Harley and my mum are standing, deep in conversation. It makes me bubble with rage and a jealousy that comes from nowhere. I knock back the rest of my wine, it's the only thing making this evening tolerable.

I hadn't realized how much I'd missed my dad's cooking or how hungry I was until his roast beef, steamed Brussels sprouts and Yorkshire pudding drizzled in gravy gets placed in front of me. It's the perfect food for such a cold and rainy day, but I can't wait for summer, for a proper South African braai. It's been too long. I crave the smokiness from flavored chicken wings, the raw meat slapped onto the grill and huge bowls of potato salad. I'm been living back in a country that's a danger to my weight, but it's so good that I don't care.

As always, my mum doesn't eat.

I don't really want to join my mother upstairs after dinner. I feel protective of my dad. Leaving Harley alone with him makes me uncomfortable, but my mother pulls me up saying she wants to show me something. Her stick-like legs sicken me as I climb the stairs behind her. Her movements are lethargic and weak without my dad there supporting her. It's hard to believe she's only in her fifties as I look at her now.

When we're inside her room, a crazy place covered with faces of cats printed on pillows, she turns to face me.

"So how're you doing?" she asks, her words slurred. She's gripping me by the shoulders. Her grotesquely long nails dig into my arms. I pull away from her.

"Fine, mum."

"Harley's lovely!" she beams.

"Yeah, she's a real gem," I say, sarcasm etched in my voice.

"Are you ever going to open up to me again?" she's swaying slightly, but I don't think she notices.

The question should evoke some sort of emotion from her, but if there's anything there I can't see it. Her eyelids sag and droop with wrinkles. Her papery skin is exquisitely thin.

"I just want my life back." It shocks me how nice it is to yield to her, to open up. It has been years since I've really spoken to her. For a moment I wonder if we could ever get back to a good place.

She laughs then, amused. I can feel my wall going right back up as my hope fades.

"That's what being a parent is about. You don't have your own life anymore."

"But I don't want to be a parent."

It looks like I've slapped her.

"I thought you wanted a family of your own? Please don't tell me you didn't?!" She speaks rapidly. The way she was looks at me scares me.

"Regan, you *need* to tell me you wanted this!" she pleads.

My gut clenches.

"Mum, what did you do?"

She changes like the flip of a switch, then. Her entire expression remolds itself to one of confusion.

"What?" she frowns.

My head is full of crazy thoughts that are impossible to believe.

"Did you do something to Peyton?" I ask. My face is deadpan but my heart has done a nosedive.

"What're you *talking* about?" her words blur together. She pushes past me with a surprising amount of force. I'm left alone in her bedroom with a million cat eyes staring back at me.

I try to get the idea of my mother having something to do with Peyton's death out of my head all night. It's a ridiculous notion. How can I be so desperate to pin someone down to Peyton's murder that I'd consider my own mother? I look at her. She's so weak, it wasn't possible... and the woman can't even watch Titanic let alone actually commit cold-blooded murder. I start second-guessing my theory that Harley was involved in it somehow, too. I'd thought her journal was proof enough, but maybe the police and my therapist were right. Maybe she is just an angry teenager who writes disgusting things in that book. I don't know. I just need to blame someone.

I watch my mother closely. She really has lost herself somewhere down the line.

I watch Harley closely, interacting with my parent's with a smile on her face and waffling down her food.

I watch my dad closely. He looks so happy. He looks at Harley the way I've always hoped he'd look at me. With love.

Why can't I be happy, too? Why can't I be loved, too?

To say that Harley is as good as gold throughout the evening would be an understatement. It's all so incongruous and unlike the girl I know at home. No matter what I say or do now, no one will believe me. The thought unnerves me as we drive home later that night.

"That was really nice," she says, staring out at the trees whizzing past us.

"It was," I reply. It wasn't.

"I'm staying late after school tomorrow. I'm doing this big project for science with a couple of friends."

"Good. I have another interview in the afternoon anyway. Can one of them give you a lift home?" I refrain from making a snarky comment about her actually having friends. She hasn't seen them much since she'd moved in and I've been starting to wonder why.

"Sure," she mutters, still staring out of the window.

◊

It's back into my interview attire the next afternoon. I'm having a small glass of wine to ease my nerves. Interviews have always given me the shakes, but I'm also having a drink because of Craig. I'd stared at my phone all morning hoping he'd text me. I don't want to visit him at the bar again, worried to appear too needy. I have no idea what we are anyway, so I don't know why I've been expecting to hear from him. I enjoyed his attention so much, I wanted more of it. I think about sending him a message but every time I start one I taper off. I have no idea what to say. What the therapist had said about me liking the idea of a relationship kept ringing in my ears. Maybe he's right.

I'm busy trying to burn off the loose threads from the seam of my skirt when I hear the floorboards creak from another room. The cats asleep under the kitchen table. When I hear another creak, I stop. My hand is suspended in the air holding onto the lighter. There's someone inside.

I hear dragging footsteps, heavy breathing.

"Harley?" It has to be her. She's supposed to be at school for a couple of hours still. I wait for a response, but nothing comes. Thoughts of getting stabbed in the stomach like Peyton whirl through my mind. I look around me; exchanging the lighter for the biggest knife I can find. It's cold and horrifying in my hands. I consider screaming, raising some sort of alarm, but I'm frozen. Panic has taken over, my body trembling with fear and adrenalin.

"Harley? If that's you, stop freaking me out!" I call once I've found my voice. It stirs the cat awake who looks at me with irritation. The bell on her collar chimes as she stretches lazily.

Everything goes quiet as I edge my way into the hallway, my legs leaden.

There's a crash and the sound of glass smashing comes from my bedroom. I jump in fright.

Slumping to the floor I hold onto my knees. I'm so sure someone is going to come out of my room and gut me. I don't know why I do it, but I start calling out Sean's name. I sob, cradling my body as I rock back and forth in fear and confusion.

When I've calmed down, I'm still not able to move. I stay in a bundle on the floor, guarding my bedroom door with the knife wedged between my knees. I lose track of the time as the silence of the house envelopes me. Daylight fades and eventually, so do I.

I wake what must be hours later, to Harley hovering over me.

"Regan?" she whispers hesitantly, looking between me and the knife. My head aches and the lights she's switched on blind me. I push myself up from off of the floor, my entire body protesting. She's still watching me as I limp to my bedroom door with dead legs. I push the door open and peer into the room. There's nothing there.

Harley follows me as I walk through to the bathroom. The photograph of Peyton and I has fallen from the windowsill. The glass smashed and scattered all across the tiles.

Harley stares at the picture of me and her mother, not saying a word.

I do a thorough search of the house as Harley stares at me like I've lost my mind. When I'm finally satisfied that no one else is here, I double check the locks. As I'm doing this we both freeze as we hear steps from outside.

"Hello?" I call. The footsteps stop for a moment, then I hear the sound of feet drag across the gravel.

"I'm calling the cops!" I yell with my eyebrows knitted together in panic.

"Stop being so dramatic," Harley rolls her eyes and stomps outside. I follow after her, surprised by her bravery.

It's the landlord. She looks terrible.

"Can I help you?" I ask her, feeling irritated that she's wondering around outside. It may be her property but this is a complete invasion of my privacy.

"Sorry dears, I'm just searching for Jasper."

It takes me a moment to remember Jasper is her cat.

"He still hasn't turned up?" Harley asks and I think to myself it's the first time I've heard concern etched in her voice. It's so unlike her that for a brief moment it completely derails me.

"No he hasn't. This isn't like him at all."

"I'll let you know if we spot him at all," I nod and usher Harley back inside. The last thing I need is to have that old bat hanging around the cottage more often. I need to establish boundaries with her.

"Can we have dinner now?" Harley asks me cautiously. I look at her for a long moment, thinking again of how I've just missed another interview.

"Sure," I say, walking into the kitchen. I pull a wine glass from the cupboard and go to find the magnum sized bottle I'd opened earlier, thoughts of Jasper already fading away. The bottle of wine is almost finished already. I have no recollection of having had that much to drink.

8

I get the earliest doctor's appointment that I can. I've been on anxiety medication and anti-depressants before but when the doctor suggested mood stabilizers on top of them, I was shocked. I hand the prescription over to the pharmacist diffidently, knowing everyone in the chemist could recognize me and the pills they're giving me. I shift my weight from foot to foot as I pay, keeping my head down.

It feel like I'm missing chunks of my days. I can't even remember driving into town this morning and it takes me a while to find my car in the parking lot. I tear my fingers through my knotted hair, squeezing at my building headache. I've been tired from the lack of sleep before, but now I'm exhausted from too much sleep. My eyes are sore, swollen and bloodshot. I hide them from myself behind a pair of sunglasses. I can't stand the sight of my reflection. I looked like my mother and I sound like her too. The doctor diagnoses me with chronic depression and an anxiety disorder making me believe everyone is responsible for Peyton's death. I try to believe it's that simple; that a packet of pills can fix me, but I still feel uneasy about Harley and my mother.

I've also just heard that Sean is back in South Africa for his holiday. The holiday we were supposed to come on together. We had planned it out perfectly. Spear-fishing, nights away on safari, road-tripping back to Jeffrey's Bay for surfing. I'd been so excited for it months ago. Now it makes me queasy knowing that he'll be so close to me. I wonder if his new girlfriend will be joining him for the trip. The thought of bumping into them is too much for me to handle. I keep scanning the faces in the crowds as I walked through the shopping center. Once or twice I'm certain I see the back of his dirty blonde hair or a flash of his face. He'll be here for just over a month and I know I'll have to become a recluse. Avoid any chance of seeing them. God knows what I'd do if I did...

When my phone buzzes and I see Craig's name on the screen, my interest piques.

Sorry I haven't been in touch. Lost your number and wasn't sure if coming over was a good idea... how are you?

His message revives me somehow. The explanation is so plausible, why had I been so upset? Of course he doesn't want to come over right away, not after the little performance Harley put on. He must be just as embarrassed as her.

I tell myself I need a harder shell as I start my engine and head home. I don't want to respond to him right away. I'm still quite out of sorts by my prescription.

I've promised myself I'm going to slow down on the booze but pour some vodka into a glass as soon as I get home. I don't know how to describe it. I have good intentions of staying away from the drink but when I walk in I took myself to the bottle automatically. I didn't think about doing it. It just happens. I slip the bottle inside of the telescope by the window to hide it from Harley. I'm sure she's getting into my stash somehow. There's absolutely no way I could be drinking as much as my bottles suggest.

I sit at the table in the kitchen, spreading the packets of medicine around me. I've worked so hard to get off of them before, but now I admit defeat.

I have to start cooking dinner for Harley soon, but before I do I press out my first round of pills, swigging them down with the warm vodka.

There's a few ingredients missing for the curry I want to make. I resent having to head back into town but have no choice. I walk, not feeling confident enough in my driving as the pills started to have a debilitating effect. I'm irritated that I've made an effort in my appearance before leaving the house. In case I bump into Sean. He's been on my mind all day.

I've managed to find his new girlfriend online and it's like a punch in the stomach. She's everything that I'm not nor could ever be. Spanish, long balyage hair, tan and dark eyes. Most of her photographs on Instagram are of her ass, which looks incredibly firm and flawless in her miniscule Brazillian bikini.

Comparing us is laughable. I feel so disgusted in myself, at my flabby stretch-marked legs getting shoved miserably into a pair of baggy, bohemian pants before the trek to town.

I detour passed the bar on the way back home. My legs carry me there without me telling them to. Craig gives me a titillating smile and holds onto my waist; trailing kisses along my jawline.

"I got your message," I said, enjoying the feeling of his hands on me. Everything was OK again. I still didn't know what we were, but it felt good.

I wasn't used to the whole 'dating' thing. I'd been in long-term relationships for as long as I could remember, so the uncertainty of this did niggle at me. I didn't want to be one of many girls. I also wanted Sean to catch wind that I'd moved on, too. It sounded petty, but having him know I wasn't pining over him anymore would knock his narcissistic ass off-kilter. It would shock him, and I'd paid to see the expression on his face when he found out he didn't have control over me anymore.

I told myself to stop thinking about things so much and to just enjoy the moment. So I did. There was a comfortable silence as we touched each other. I nipped him gently on the lips, making him pull me closer to him. The medicine made me light on my feet and giggly.

"I like these," he tugged at my pants and I felt my confidence levels rising already.

"I just wanted to come and say hi," I said after a few minutes.

"Hi," he kissed my earlobe.

"Let's do something soon," I say, looking up at his bearded face.

"How about I give you a night off from the kitchen soon? I can take you out for dinner."

"I think I'm free on Wednesday," I smile. My face feels slightly numb.

"I wasn't aware I was going to have to pay for you!" he jokes. I try to laugh and keep steady, to control my facial features but I can feel myself slipping away. I pull away from him, picking up the shopping bags and shouting from over my shoulder that he should call me as I try my best to walk away in a straight line.

I get away from him as quickly as I can so that he doesn't see me in the state I'm in. The booze and pills swirl around in my head, making me unable to walk in a straight line. I lose myself in the throng of people bustling past me in town. By the time I finally reach the cottage, I can hardly remember the walk. Harley's bedroom light is on and there's music blaring out from her open window. I groan, unlocking the front door and dropping the grocery bags onto the kitchen counter.

I call to her, telling her to turn the music down but she can't hear me. I roll my eyes, tripping over a cat toy on my way down the hallway to her room. The door is slightly ajar. I know then that something is wrong. She always locks the door behind her.

"Harley?" I call again, pushing the door wide open. All I see is a mess of sun-bleached hair, dark legs wrapped around broad shoulders. Her supple body writhes beneath him with fluid movements.

I howl.

◊

I rip Sean off of Harley, pummeling his bare, hairy chest with my fists.

He looks so surprised to see me in her room. His sweaty hands that have just been all over Harley's body grab my wrists, restraining me. I fight against him, kicking at his cock that is still rock hard and covered in latex.

"Regan, calm the fuck down!" he shouts above my screaming. It looks like he's trying not to laugh. I'm humiliated. This is all a big joke to him.

I can't speak. I can't breathe. I can't even see as I tear my hand free from his grasp and connect my fist into his face. I don't think it's a very hard punch. I've never hit anybody before, but I gave it my all. My knuckles feel instantly bruised and swollen. Harley scrambles under her sheets, staring at us wide-eyed.

"Get out of my house," I wail at both of them, collapsing to the floor as Sean drops me to inspect his face in Harley's mirror.

"You fucking crazy bitch!" he shouts at me. His familiar deep voice rings through my throbbing eardrums. I feel like I'm right back in Spain and it triggers me into a full blown panic.

"I'm crazy!? You're the one that's just screwed a thirteen year old girl, you sick *fuck*!" I gasp between sobs. I feel so exposed and shattered. I can't believe what I've just walked in on. Sean. My Sean. The Sean I'd loved and the Sean who had ripped my heart out, fucking my Godchild. I gag and wretch on the bedroom floor as I fight to clear the images from my head.

"What?! She told me she's nineteen," Sean says, his eyes darting from me to her.

Harley remains silent.

"Sean you're a forty year old man. *Look* at her! She's not nineteen!" I spit in his face, throwing his discarded clothes at him, then I turn to Harley.

"Get out of my house right now!" I snarl at her, gripping the bed sheets and pulling them away from her. I start destroying her room, pushing everything that has been on her desk onto the floor. I rip down posters and throw books from the shelving. I'm in such a blind rage that I pull her lamp right out of the socket and fling it at Sean's head. In this moment, I wanted to kill them both.

"This is a madhouse!" he yells as he buckles his belt.

"I came here to see you. I got your address from someone in town and when Harley opened the door she said you were out. She said I could wait for you if I wanted to and then she fucking seduced me!" I want to block out his voice. I don't want to hear anything he has to say or let him infect my life again, but I can't stop myself from barking back at him.

"That's right; it's never your fault is it?! You can't keep your dick in your pants, Sean!" I vomit, and then everything around me fades away.

When I wake up, the house is quiet. I feel awful; groggy. I'm in my bed, but I can't remember how I got here. I try to think. Flashbacks of Sean with Harley are so hazy that I question if I'd dreamt it all. Could the pills have allowed me such vivid dreams?

I lift myself from the bed reluctantly and creep through the cottage. Harley's room is immaculate; cleaner than I've ever seen it even before she moved in. There's a light on in the kitchen so I make my way there. My vision is blurry but I can see a figure standing by the sink. The water is running.

"What are you doing?" I croak. My throat hurts, as if I've been screaming. I'm just starting to piece things together when Harley turns to face me, a knife in her hands. Soap slides down the handle and drops from the tip of the knife onto the kitchen floor.

"Oh good, you're up. I made dinner," she says with a smile, sauntering up to me, preying on my weakness. There's a repulsive smell in the air.

She's dressed up again, wearing a small black dress. It takes me a moment to recognize it. It's mine. It's the dress I'd worn to her mother's funeral.

"Harley, why are you dressed like that?" my voice is thick with sleep.

"Regan, you have the most beautiful daughter in the world," Harley whispers then, running her wet fingers across my trembling lips. Her breath is hot against my face.

9

Any trace of Sean being in the house has been removed. It's like he has never been here at all. Only when I'm taking out the rubbish do I notice a used condom pour out with the contents from the kitchen dustbin. There are traces of brown blood along the latex and while I can't remember having bled during sex with Craig, it could easily be his. I shudder, wondering if I should unblock Sean and ask, but if it has been a dream it would sound too crazy. I feel crazy. The only thing I have to go on are the bruises around my wrists, marks all too similar to me when it comes to Sean. I poke at them tenderly, willing myself to remember anything for certain.

I'm hysterical when my dad calls to ask if we'd like to come over for a visit. He never used to invite me over; I know it's all about Harley now.

"Regan," my dad says from down the phone line. He can't make out a word I'm saying.

"Calm down. Tell me what's wrong?"

His voice is gentle but firm at the same time. It's a sound I love and I clutch onto the phone, wishing he were here.

I tell him. I tell him everything and when I'm finished, he sighs.

"Dad?" I ask hesitantly. I hear him clear his throat and shift positions.

"Regan, darling, are you back on medication?"

My stomach churns and twists at his question. Why would he ask me that?

"Dad, I'm not crazy." I don't know if I'm trying to convince him, or myself.

"Answer the question."

I tell him that I am and I can actually hear his relief. It confuses me, making me dizzy. I can't understand what's going on.

He has one of his hourly coughing fits down the phone, the joys of being a chain-smoker. I wait for it to subside, staring blankly at the raindrops sliding down the windowsill.

"What would happen if I didn't want her, dad?" I ask when things went quiet, feeling guilt-ridden for asking. Peyton would be turning in her grave right now.

"That doesn't matter. She is your responsibility now, Regan. You need to stop running away from your problems. It's time you grew up." I hear the click of his lighter, a pull on a cigarette and a long exhale.

I can't help but wonder if he's talking about more than just Harley. Looking back on my life, I've run away from everything eventually. I've left boyfriend after boyfriend the second things got too serious, or at least found a way to mess things up irreparably. Peyton used to laugh at me, tell me I had commitment issues. I never believed her until now. Now, everything hits me all at once.

I don't know why I am the way that I am. So many people around me make it work. They're all holding together relationships, buying houses, getting married, having children. It just never seems to be in the cards for me. A part of me doesn't want it, yet another part of me does and whenever I come close to getting it, I run for the hills. I wish I understood myself better. I wish I wasn't just one big contradiction.

The only person I've ever tried to make it go the distance with is Sean but part of that was because I was too scared to leave him. Either way you look at it, I seem like a coward.

I cancel my date with Craig, promising to make it up to him another time. After Harley's vile concoction in the kitchen I'm looking forward to some more of my dad's cooking.

She becomes this malleable angel once again as soon as we arrive at their door. There's no real need to set the scene for you. Drunken mother, delightful Godchild; it could be a reenactment of the other evening. The only unique event is when my parent's dog growls as we step into the house. Harley and I are standing so close together that I can't tell if he's being hostile to her, or me, which was crazy. That dog has always loved me, but tonight, his hair spiked up on his neck and back. He bares his teeth and lets out low, angry grumbles and I can't seem to shake the feeling that he's been staring at me while he growls.

It was over dinner, chicken casserole, when my dad takes Harley's hand and makes a suggestion.

"Why don't you come and spend some time with us, Harley?"

I don't know what to do or say. I don't want her anywhere near my parents, but the time without her would be blissful. Harley answers with tears before I have a chance to intervene.

"Why doesn't Regan want me?" She puts it so bluntly, it shocks us all.

My mother rushes to her side and drapes herself over her shoulders like a blanket.

"Oh honey, it isn't that she doesn't want you!" my mum coos, shooting daggers at me with her eyes.

I can't understand how they don't see the manipulation. It's so evident.

"She's right. It's just that we want more time with you," my dad tells her, heading over to Harley and patting her arm. She pulls away from him.

"Please don't touch me," she begs, shaking. My dad draws his hand away quickly, looking uncomfortable. Now that I think about it, she hasn't really warmed to my dad at all over our evenings together. I stare at her curiously, wondering why.

Harley sniffs, staring down at her plate of food. She allows my mother to comfort her. My dad stands close by, but doesn't touch her again.

Even the dog who has been comatose under the table shoves his wet nose into Harley's lap. My side of the table is suddenly empty.

"My mummy wanted me to be with Regan," she says. Her voice quivers. It sounds young, immature. What thirteen year-old still called their mother, 'mummy?'

"Well, we'd still love to have you if you do change your mind," my mother smiles reassuringly.

"Pl-please don't make me live here," she stutters through sobs. She looks frightened. I can do nothing but sit here, chewing incessantly on a strip of chicken.

"You're going to have to start trying a bit harder, Regan," my dad pipes up, in front of everyone. The way he looks at me breaks my heart. It's a look of disappointment. I swallow the chicken and start tearing the skin from the inside of my cheek. I grind my teeth so hard that everyone can hear the creaking as I move my jaw back and forth. They look repulsed. My dad asks me to stop.

"Look at her, poor thing," my mum pouts down to Harley, still holding onto her.

"She needs stability; a loving home. You're all she's got, Regan," dad says, shaking his head, berating me.

I see Harley glance up at me. She gives me the same blood-chilling look I'd seen the night she'd walked in on Craig and I in my bed. My parents are too busy to notice.

I get up and head for the guest bathroom to splash cold water in my face. It must have been a trick of the light. I must be imagining things. It's my anxiety, it has to be. I haven't taken my pills yet, that's why I'm seeing Harley looking at me so strangely.

I punch my doses out of the packaging and wash them down with tap water, hoping they'll put me at ease. One of the pills gets lodged in the back of my throat. I choke, gulping down more water. When I emerge from the toilet, I find Harley and my parent's conferring urgently in hushed tones.

"What're you guys talking about?" I frown.

"Nothing," my mother says, a little too quickly for my liking.

I can still feel the pill trying to work its way down my throat. It almost makes me gag.

I could be wrong, but I'm certain I heard Harley say something like 'I don't want to make Auntie Regan angry again...' just before I walk into the room... she looks so frightened as she said it. She's trying to turn my own family against me, I know it.

*

When my parent's clear the plates away, I round on Harley.

"I'm onto you," I whisper to her from across the table. She gives me an innocent look.

"What do you mean?" She blinks; her long lashes fluttering irritatingly on her high cheekbones.

I get up and walk over to her. I don't know what comes over me but I grab her by the wrists and pulled her up. Her chair falls backwards and lands with a harsh thud onto the floor. I catch a glimpse of myself in the mirror, my features are ravaged. I don't look like myself.

"The manipulation isn't going to work!" I say, my voice frothing venomously. I shake her, hard. She tries reeling back but it only makes my grip on her tighten.

"Regan, stop! Please. You're hurting me!" she cries, loud enough for my parent's to hear. I don't stop. Every little thing that's been building up comes out as I seize her; rattling her bony body in my hands. She weighs nothing. She's just a bag of bones. Her head lolls around uncontrollably as I assail her, lacerating her arms with my fingernails. I don't even notice when my parents run back into the room.

Before I know what's happening, my dad throws me off of her and I hurtle across the room. Shock hits me as I slam into a wall at full speed. There's so much adrenalin coursing through me, I can't even remember what I've said to her or what I've done. The medicine is making me drowsy already. I'm sweating alcohol.

Harley buckles to her knees, holding her forearms.

There are angry red welts up her arms from where I've grabbed her. She's crying.

"I think you should go, Regan," my mother slurs. She tries to look panicked but in her drunken state she just appears crazy. The tension in the room is palpable.

I can't believe it. My own parents are kicking me out of their house.

"No, please!" Harley interrupts. We all look at her.

"I don't want to be an inconvenience to anyone," she says.

I don't remember even knowing the definition of inconvenience when I was her age. Her childish voice has been replaced. She suddenly seems like an entirely different person. She suddenly reminds me more of Peyton than ever before.

Harley and I are put inside my car very reluctantly by my parent's. I can tell they don't want us to be alone together. I don't want to be us to be alone together either, but it seems once again I have no choice.

As we drive, I break the silence.

"You did that on purpose," I state. She's quiet for a while then turns to face me. Her eyes gleam in the moonlight.

"I'd be more careful around me if I were you. I know all of your filthy little secrets, remember?"

I don't know what she's talking about.

I don't know anything anymore.

10

I can't sleep. Her words stay with me all night, possessing me. She knows all of my filthy little secrets. I don't know if she's referring to Craig, or something else. I can't imagine what else there could be, yet I feel exposed. I feel like I've done something that she can use against me, but I have no idea what it could be. The guilt radiates from me but I don't understand why. She is so tactful and manipulative; I've never met anyone quite like her before. The effect she has on me is powerful.

At breakfast the next morning I tell Harley to leave her room unlocked. When she asks me why, she looks scared; defensive. I tell her I need to clean it. God knows she won't sweep up or change her own bedding.

Entering her room again is like entering a different world. Although this is my cottage, her room seems detached from the rest of the house. It's cold, derelict. I feel like an unwanted, unwelcome intruder. Her energy lingers in the room long after she's left. It vibrates an abnormal darkness that overwhelms me, making me leave the room a number of times just to be able to breathe again. Inside Harley's room, my chest closes up. The walls seem to be caving in on me. It's too quiet, somehow blocking any noise made outside of it. There's also some kind of dry rot spreading in the corner. As expected, the room is a tip. I wonder if she purposefully made a bigger mess of it before she left for school. I get down on my hands and knees, peeling discolored socks and scrunched up dirty knickers from off of the floorboards. When I shove a load of laundry in to wash, I go on a bit of a cleaning frenzy. I want to do Harley's room first so that I know I have sufficient time there while she's out. Her journal isn't where I'd found it before, nor is it anywhere else in her cluttered mess of a room. She must have taken it with her. I not expecting to find anything else in the room so I'm not sure what drives me to lift up the rug. Usually, I'd have just swept around it, but today I want to clean everything. I want to disinfect the room of Harley. I'm going to take the rug out and bash the dust from it but when I see what's underneath it I dropped it in horror.

◊

I don't know how long it has been there, but the shirt is creased and the blood has turned the material stiff as a board. Smears coat it front and back. It's a shirt that would drown Harley if she wore it. There's something heavy wrapped inside of it but I'm trembling so much it takes me a while to open it up. When it slips from the hardened fabric, I manage to grab it before it lands on the floor but as soon as I see it, I dropped it like it's burnt me. I gasp but can't keep hold of any air. I begin hyperventilating, my heart rate thundering dangerously as I stare down at the bloody, serrated blade. It has a black handle that must be at least thirty centimeters long. My fingerprints would be all over it, now.

I don't know what to do. Part of me wants to fall to my knees and cradle the crusty shirt. It's Peyton's blood. It's Peyton. Tears fall freely around me. I can't even think of what to do. I can't think at all.

When I finally let my eyes leave the knife and rumpled shirt, I see a side plate on Harley's dressing table. Crumbs from something she's eaten scatter the porcelain. I let the crumbs fall onto the freshly swept floors. My legs feel heavy as I pull myself towards the knife. I slip the plate beneath it, too afraid to touch it again even though it's already too late.

The plate slots into the cupboard behind a packet of Cheerio's where I leave it for the rest of the day. I clean the rest of the house in a daze, barely aware of anything.

I spend the last lick of freedom for the day down at Craig's bar. I want to tell him what I've found, ask him for advice, but I can't get the words out. It's impossible to describe just how frightened I am; although I'm sure he can sense it as I nurse a glass of wine thirstily. Every time he tries to talk to me, I'm so wrapped up in my own world that I don't even hear him. I apologize but can clearly see that he's annoyed. I would be too, but I have a dozen scenarios flying around in my head. If I take that knife and shirt to the police, they would be covered in my prints. Would they arrest me until I was proven innocent? Would Harley's prints be on there, too? Who were the cops likely to believe, me or her?

I could throw them away, but where? Someone somehow would unearth them. Then what? I could burn the shirt but the knife was a different story – and why would I tamper with evidence? I wasn't guilty... but I had been rattled by the interrogation before. This would probably give the police even more suspicion against me. I have no idea who to could go to for help. My dad would think I'm mad; in fact I'm fairly certain he already does. Craig would probably go running. I can already tell that we're on different pages. He's trying to be so attentive and affectionate but my mind is elsewhere. I stare at him, this incredibly handsome man that I know I don't deserve. One part of me feels like the luckiest girl in the world that someone like him was even remotely interested in someone like me, the other part of me feels sorry for him. He could do so much better than me. He could have absolutely any girl he wanted. A blonde, with bigger breasts and bluer eyes; someone more toned and tanned. He's so different from anyone I'd ever been with before, especially Sean. He's incredibly gentle and doting. After Sean I guess I've become used to being handled a bit rougher and admittedly, a big part of me did miss a hard slap on the ass from time to time. Part of me loves having my body rough-housed as they say. I'm just not used to how soft he is with me, or how much he listens. It makes me feel special in a way I've never had before. He's genuinely concerned about me now and I can't even give him my full attention.

"I'm sorry, Craig. I just have a lot going on right now," I rub his hand from across the bar. As always, he understands.

"I need to get home before Harley, make sure dinners going and help her with her homework, but can I call you later?" I don't know why I say I'm going to help Harley with her homework. I've never done so before and I'm certainly not about to start. It's just another fabrication that seemed to slip out. I couldn't stop it.

Harley has an inexorable penchant for wrecking whatever nerves I have left. The way she boorishly slices her carving of beef makes me uneasy. I find myself unable to take my eyes from her hand wrapped around the knife. I know that it's now or never. I slide my chair back and leave the table. Harley barely acknowledges my movement. I slither my way hesitantly through the cramped kitchen that had once felt so spacious. Slowly but surely it seems that Harley is commandeering my entire cottage.

"Harley," I say. My voice is tentative. There's no response from her; just the sound of her chewing, working her jaw, crunching on the undercooked vegetables.

"We need to talk," I walk up behind her and slip the side plate holding the bloody knife in front of her.

She swallows, meat slowly working its way down her slender little throat. Her eyes remain cast down onto the plate, but it's impossible to know what's going through her mind.

I move to the side so I can get a better look at her. I can see hundreds of fine little hairs bristle on her top lip as her mouth twitches.

"Harley, is this a sick joke?" I ask beseechingly. It's the only other explanation I have. It was this, or Harley really had killed her own mother.

She gives me a wry look as she lifts her head, running her tongue across her teeth.

"If you know something you need to tell me," I feel as though I'm speaking to a brick wall. I want to change tact. Perhaps if she thinks I don't suspect her she'll open up.

My mobile phone is recording the conversation in my back pocket. If I can just get a confession or something out of her I could take it to the police.

Instead, she smiles, almost sadly. "I think we both know what happened that night, don't we?"

The way she plays these riddles and parries my questions infuriates me. The somber look in her eyes confuses and unhinges me. I can't take it anymore. My hand meets her face with a loud clap. My open palm stings from the impact. She looks genuinely shocked, her dark brown eyes well with tears she refuses to spill. She draws in a deep breath, flaring her nostrils as her cheek start to redden. I can see my fingers outlined in her complexion.

I can't move. Adrenaline and anger courses through my body. Fear gnaws at me but I am unrepentant. Harley slams her cutlery down so hard that I jump. For a moment I think she's going to combust. Scream, wail, cry; yet she remains as silent as ever. That's what worries me the most, her silence. Her composure. Brief spurts of fury or surprise but nothing more.

She takes one last lascivious look at me, then leaves the room.

I'm glued to the spot, too afraid to move. The plate with the bloody blade stares at me hauntingly. I can't piece anything together anymore. Nothing makes any sense. I've been trying so hard to avoid the bottle of wine calling my name. The limpid liquid is too enticing to ignore. I clutch onto the stem of the wine glass like it's my protection as I swallow down my pills. I finish the last of the white, and then uncork a red I'd forgotten I'd bought.

I swirl the full-bodied liquid around in my mouth and coat my throat with its spiciness. My tension eases almost instantly.

The phone is still wedged into my back pocket. I pull it out hastily and stop the recording, deleting the file. I have nothing worth producing to the police. I'm starting to doubt that I ever will. There's a message from Craig, asking if I'm OK. I text back:

I'd be better if you were here with me. Inside me.

Despite everything, I'm horny. His reply is quick.

You sure it's OK to cum over?

I grin at his misspelling but feel irritated by his question at the same time. I resent Harley then. Maybe it's the booze taking effect, but I suddenly feel more confident. This is my house, I should be allowed to have guests over whenever I feel like it.

It's OK.

I wait. When my phone beeps with another message, I smile. Aroused.

Be right there.

*

Craig sneaks in quietly and in the darkness of my bedroom I remove his shirt. I pull it off over his head and press my body up against him, feeling his warmth. For once, the house is still. No creaking floorboards or groaning geysers, just the sound of our breathing as we connect.

As soon as he's on top of me, I feel safer. Secure. I think of him as my shield.

He pushes inside of me, filling me up and making me whole.

I never want him to leave.

11

I'm parched, with a raging headache coming on as I shuffle Craig out of the cottage surreptitiously the next morning. I'm secretly glad he doesn't want to stay for coffee, I'd forgotten to buy milk again, distracted by the wine aisle. Again.

I've barely slept all night, enjoying the sound of his heavy breathing beside me too much. I stayed up staring at my ceiling, trying to figure out what to do with the shirt and knife. I think I've finally come up with a plan.

I call my parent's home phone, hoping to get through to my dad but it's my mother's airy voice drifting through the speaker.

"I need you to look after Harley tonight," I say, getting right to the point. She sounds so cavalier as she agrees to have her over.

The journey to the house is awkward. Harley and I haven't said a word to each other since I'd slapped her. I know she thinks we're both going over to my folks for the day. She can't believe it when I drop her off.

"Where are you going?" she demands, wide-eyed.

"I have some things to take care of. Alone," I tell her, trying to gauge her reaction. Before I can, my mother tiptoes up behind her and grabs her by the shoulders. It makes her jump. I wonder why she's so nervous.

"Should I make enough dinner for you, too?" Mum asks me. I hate that she's made it sound like she'd be doing the cooking when we all know it's always my dad.

"No, I might only be back tomorrow morning," I say.

"That's my wayward daughter," my dad says as he joins us in the driveway. I'm fairly certain his comment hadn't been said in jest but I try to laugh it off. He slips me some money discreetly. It humiliates me that I'd had to ask him for a loan to be able to afford fuel for my trip. I need to get a job as soon as possible.

Before Harley can say anything, I drive off.

My boot is loaded with the basic camping equipment; a tent, sleeping bag, gas burner, a pot and an old mug missing its handle. The knife I'd found underneath Harley's rug is wrapped up in the shirt and tucked under the front seat. I need to get rid of them. I need to dispel my anxiety of being caught with them in my home.

The drive takes longer than expected. I keep casting fevered glances over my shoulder; certain Harley was going to find a way to follow me.

I relax eventually, cracking my neck and loosening my grip on the steering wheel, leaving civilization behind. The roads slowly turn to dirt and I kick up dust as I venture further into the forest. Small snakes slither frantically across the trail to get out of my way. The trees hang heavily overhead, blocking out the sunlight. The shade makes it seem much later than it is. It won't be long until I'll have to light a fire.

I purposefully didn't bring along a bottle of wine. I hate to admit it but I feel so much more in control and focused without it here and I need that right now.

As soon as I manage to steer off of the pot-hole ridden road, I park up in a clearing in the forest and get started on a fire.

It's overwhelmingly quiet out here. No rumbling car engines or children's' screeching laughter. No hustle and bustle from neighbors or a blaring television you can't turn down. It's so tranquil... I love it. But then, I've always been one for silence and solitude. There's only the sound of the water flowing down the gully to keep me company, along with the trees fringing my campsite. Knowing that I'm far away from Harley makes the isolation enjoyable, almost addictive. It reminds me that I don't need to feel safe in Craig's arms because I feel perfectly fine alone. I guess some people would find being out here in a forest all alone daunting. Not me. I need this from time to time; space from the rest of the world. With the fire roaring to life, I unwrap the knife and placed it on a tree stump beside me. My breath frosts as I exhale, holding the blood stained shirt out in front of the fire. I say a prayer, to who I don't know... but I say one anyway; for Peyton.

The shirt is sucked away into plumes of smoke, the flames turning it into a pile of grey ash. It makes me feel lighter already, until I pick up the knife. This was going to be harder to dispose of.

I touch the tip of the blade, letting it break the skin of my fingertip. I twist it around in my hands for what could have been hours as I rack my brain for ideas.

Once again I consider turning it in to the police. It has Peyton's DNA on it and I do have a solid alibi for the night of her murder thanks to my landlord. But I've tampered with evidence now.

I'm not very clued up when it comes to the law. Peyton was always the one more obsessed with true crime podcasts than me. Still, I'm pretty sure that tampering with evidence would be reason enough to arrest me. I can't let that happen. I won't let it.

Burying the knife would be fine for now but eventually, inevitably, someone would unearth it. It would be tied back to me, I know it would. I'm stuck with it.

Mosquito's buzz around me hungrily, attracted by both the fire and the smell of my warm, sweet blood. When one lands on my arm, I let it drink from me for a while. Then, very carefully with my other hand, I pinch my skin together around the area of skin the mosquito was sitting. The pressure of so much blood makes them unable to pull out and they just keep filling up until they burst. I let that happen. I don't know why it made me feel good, but it did... even when my arm begins to swell and itch from the poison it left behind.

I'm in my own world, lapping up the heat from the fire and playing curiously with the knife when my phone rings. It gives me a fright as I'd been certain there wasn't any signal out here. You can never escape reality, I guess.

"Regan, you need to get back here right now. It's Harley," my father cries down the phone. His voice is barely audible over the sound of screaming in the background.

I have no idea what to expect when I arrive. Harley is incoherent. She's crying hysterically.

"What's happened?!" I ask, kneeling down beside her. She's a manipulator, that's evident, but I doubt even she could be this good an actress.

"All I did was try to give her a kiss goodnight!" my mother is waving her arms about, pulling at her electrified puff of ginger hair. The dye is fading fast.

I try to reach out for Harley's hand but she rips her body away from all of us.

"Stop touching me!" she screams. Snot and tears stream down her trembling face. I've never seen her look so distraught. She's buckled over, clutching onto her knobbly knees. Words are pouring out of her but none of them make any sense.

"What's she saying?" my dad asks, hovering nearby but too afraid to come close. I shake my head in response, I have no idea.

"Should I call an ambulance?" mum asks frantically. This makes Harley sob harder. I can just make out the words, 'no, no, no...'

As her panic eventually subsides, I start piecing together more whispered words.

"Please just stop touching me..."

I was raped when I was a little girl.

To see Harley reacting in such a way to just a touch of affection paralyzes me. I haven't thought about my past for so long. It's been buried in the box I've been intending to put everything to do with Sean into.

It all hits me now, knocking the wind and life out of me.

Peyton never mentioned anything about Harley being a victim of sexual abuse. If anything, she'd have come to me.

I try telling myself that I'm reading too much into it. Sexual assault leaves you paranoid forever more. There's nothing really to suggest Harley has gone through something so traumatic. I try to think of other possibilities. I try to get *him* out of my head.

Big, warm, calloused hands around my throat. I can't breathe. I can't scream. Feeling him harden as I thrash and buck beneath him. He's getting off on me putting up a fight. I hear a violent rip as he shreds my clothing from my quivering body...

*

Maybe she's been overwhelmed by a motherly touch. There's no denying I've been an awful Godparent over the last few weeks. I've been so focused on my own grief over Peyton's death that I haven't really considered what Harley must be going through; funny how that without alcohol I seem to be able to put everything into perspective for once.

I hate myself then, knowing I've been victimizing myself and revolving everything around me. I want to change the way I am. I want to be a better, more considerate person.

Sympathy suddenly drowns me. I've been so cruel to her, my best friend's daughter!

Before I know it, I've collapsed down next to her and together we cry. Everything comes out of me at once. All of the emotions from the past few weeks: Peyton's death, the heartbreak with Sean, the fight with alcohol, the realization that I'm turning into my mother all flow out of me after vivid flashbacks of an older man being inside of a ten year old me.

I haven't cried like this since the day I'd told my mother about the rape. We'd been walking the dog down by the lagoon when she'd seen deep, jagged cuts and abrasions up both of my wrists and forearms. I'd managed to hide everything from my parents for so long and they had never once noticed my cries for help.

It felt good to let it all out at first, until I saw the way she looked at me. I have no other way to describe it other than disgust. It made me feel shameful, dirty.

I'd fallen to the damp, smelly sand and broken down that day. I'd shed tears matching the magnitude and extremity of the cries that were falling around me now all these years later.

Just like back then, my mother doesn't try to help me up or offer any form of comfort. She just stares down at me in wonderment, too lost in her own alcohol riddled world to really understand what's going on around her. Doctors say it isn't her fault at this stage; that it's turned into a disease. Yet I blame her for so much and right now I feel like I've lost my mother too. Just like Harley.

I can almost hear my mother's thoughts as she stares down at me: *how can this possibly be my daughter?*

At seeing my breakdown, Harley's cries ease to small whimpers. She wipes her nose up her arm, leaving a long slimy trail up her skin.

"I don't know why *you're* crying," she spits. I look at her, bewildered.

An apology for the way I've been treating her is definitely warranted, but I don't know how to do it. I've become so used to resenting her now that changing my mindset is difficult.

Despite everything, there are still unexplainable things that make me scared of her. She won't talk to me either, so I'm at a complete loss.

"Why don't you just go? Leave me here like you planned. Go fuck your new boyfriend or something," she says sharply.

"You have another boyfriend?" my dad asks, grimacing. Great, all I need now is more of their unprecedented judgment. That's when Harley flicks me a vicious little snigger.

Is it possible that she could be this conniving? Leering me back home, faking some sort of a panic attack, gaining further sympathy from everyone including me!?

She shifts the focus back onto me, letting my family know about the bartender she'd caught me fucking.

"You've brought her into a disgraceful environment. This is why you have no children of your own," my mum shakes her head at me, belittling me. I want to laugh at her then. How dare she speak about disgraceful environments to me and how *dare* she use the one thing against me that she knows would rip me apart at the seams. It stings more than she could ever possibly know.

I'm not certain my mother can even remember anymore the time I had confided in her when those two faint little lines had shown up on my pregnancy test. I not certain she can remember how I'd cried, petrified by the thought of becoming a mother... to a rapist's child no less. I'd kept the baby. After days and days of trying to decide what to do, I'd come to the conclusion that it wasn't the babies fault. I decided that if I could raise the baby well, it would be nothing like its father.

It had taken me a long time to get used to the idea and as the baby grew inside of me, squirming and wriggling about, flashbacks of the night he had forced himself into me were vivid and impossible to stop. My only hope was that it looked nothing like him. His features constantly haunted me. I could remember every miniscule detail about him. The small brown mole on the side of his chin. The slanted smirk he couldn't wipe from his face from the moment I'd opened the front door to the moment he'd left me cowering in a corner, bound and broken.

The miscarriage had been brutal and my life had been pillaged. Pushing her tiny, not yet fully-formed lifeless body out of me was the most shocking, macabre surprise of my life.

Not only had it devastated me, it had also relieved me and that alone was enough to make me want to die. How could I feel two such polar opposite, intense emotions at once? I'd slipped into such a deep, dark depression and I still have the scars snaking across my wrists to prove it. I finger them now as I think of the shoe box beneath my bed. Tiny pink shoes and Winnie the Pooh pacifiers, ultrasound scans and dozens of baby girls outfits now gathering dust. I haven't looked inside that box in years, but it's never far away from me. I'd loved that little girl already, more than anything else in the world. She wasn't a rapists baby... she'd been my baby; my Hannah.

I draw in a breath, biting the inside of my cheek. I tear off a thick chunk of flesh and play with the soggy skin with my tongue. I realize then that I haven't taken my medication for the evening.

I take one long look right into my mother's eyes, willing her to remember... and walk away.

I cannot believe I almost felt sorry for her. I laugh as I wash my pills down with a glass of wine in the bathroom. I need the wine and I need the privacy. The bathroom echoes around me, the cold white walls making me feel like I'm in some sort of an asylum. *Maybe I should be...* I drink one glass after another, cradling the glass with the bottle clasped firmly between my thighs. I dive into a packet of my dad's cigarettes, exhaling through the crack in the window. I'd nicked them from him long after he'd passed out in his armchair.

I can't drive home in this state, so instead Harley and I stay for the night. I'm actually quite happy with a seemingly endless supply of booze. I did try to stop drinking but as stress built up around me and inside of me, my brain couldn't stop ticking. I couldn't stop thinking about the relief I knew it would give me as soon as I took that first sip. I don't even feel ashamed anymore.

12

"What did you do with the evidence?" her eyes glitter with curiosity. We're back home now; stuck together in my cottage. It's somehow growing smaller by the day. It's then I remember the knife, still in my possession. It's wedged between the slits in the backseat of my car. I pale. It's weighing me down so much that I can barely breathe.

I don't answer her. Instead, I break down. The tears come from nowhere; they're aggressive and relentless. Harley's hips sashay through the room but I can't make out what she's doing through my blurred vision.

She procures me to have a glass of wine. It's placed in front of me gently; the sweet aroma fills my nostrils. It gives me an instant thrill. My heart ups its pace. The need for it is suffocating.

"Take this. It will help." She speaks softly. A tiny white pill tips from her hand and lands beside my glass. I look at it skeptically.

"For your nerves," she explains. I don't know whether to trust her or not but my hand picks up the pill and I press it to my tongue. The wine definitely isn't one that I've purchased. It's revoltingly sweet; a headache waiting to happen. I wonder how she'd managed to get it, but decide not to ask questions. I drain the glass, and then look around for more. Harley drags a heavy bottle from the counter and pours me another, as though she's read my mind.

I dab at my eyes, embarrassed by how eager I am. I hate that she can tell. It's a generous amount of wine that tapers down my hysteria within seconds.

"You might as well join me. It's your wine, and apparently you're old enough to fuck my men anyway," I say defiantly, raising the glass to my lips. There's no hiding the cruelty in my voice.

She frowns, sighs and reaches for another glass from the cabinet. The sound of the wine pouring into the glass is music to my ears.

I watch as she takes a small, measured sip. She looks ridiculous; the glass bigger than her face. I snort but she doesn't seem to notice.

Shifting positions, I circle the rim of the glass with my finger, making a whistling sound. The room is awkwardly silent and I need to break it.

"Can I ask you a question?"

Harley raises her thick, bushy eyebrows at me. They're the kind that couldn't suit anyone but her.

"Why was your mum so scared of you?" It's been on my mind every day. Why had Peyton been so afraid of her in the coffee shop that day and why have I been so frightened of her ever since?

"What did you do with the knife?" she counteracts, her eyes smoldering.

I stare at her wishing I knew how this little girl seems to always have the upper hand. Even from a young age Harley had never been one to be shy. She'd never hidden behind the comforts of her mother or played coy around those new to her. She exudes confidence, so much so that at times it appears staged.

"It's in the car. I don't know what to do with it," I say, raking my fingers through greasy hair.

"I'll deal with it," she whispers with a confidence in her voice that I envy. I'm overcome with this longing to learn from her; be like her, be *liked* by her. It reminds me all too much of the acceptance I'd once been so desperate for from Peyton. Like mother like daughter. I top up both of our glasses. It feels better not to be drinking alone anyway, even if it was with someone who has just hit puberty.

I certainly not expecting to fall into such easy conversation with her. The usually tense room becomes light, breathable. She's talking a mile a minute about this and that.

She may seem old enough to shag Sean and to buy booze, but she still isn't quite old enough to be able to hold her alcohol. Neither am I it seems. I'm soon floating away, losing myself in my own words and laughter. Harley's words swallow me whole and my limbs become numb as I fall further away from myself, from reality. I barely comprehend it when she grasps my hand and tells me that we should go to the shooting range. It's like two drunken teenage boys deciding to go to a strip club. It's ludicrous, but at the time it feels like the best thing to do right now.

"We have to act sober!" I giggle, my feet clumsy and heavy.

If I was the supervisory personnel today, I would never put a gun in either of our hands. Then again, I would never go to a taxidermy ridden rifle range if was in the right frame of mind either. Harley however, as she does, gets away with it. She spins a story about me getting married. She tell the man at the range that she's my Godchild, taking me on a surprise Hen's day because I'm new here and have no friends. It's the first time that it's dawned on me that I actually don't. Not anymore anyway. I try not to let it bother me. I level the rifle, shooting at my target in the distance with the horizon changing hue behind it.

I still feel giddy when I wake, a lopsided smile on my face despite the dreams of stuffed raccoons stalking me. Drool slides down my chin; I can't be bothered to wipe it away.

I press my head into the sofa cushions, it feels comforting and warm. I could stay here all day, but a vague memory of Harley standing above me with my legs in the air suddenly comes to the forefront of my mind. I blink. Tearing the blanket from my body, I'm relieved to see that I'm clothed. I feel filthy even thinking of the alternative. A veneer of false hope washes over me for only a moment. It takes me a couple of seconds to realize I'm not wearing what I had fallen asleep in. I'm in sweatpants that I'm sure were folded up neatly in my cupboard the previous evening. Had Harley *changed* me? I don't have much time to think about the strange innuendos. A knock at the door gives me a reality check. What the *fuck* had I been doing last night? Had I seriously been drinking with a minor? With *Harley*? I had once joked with Peyton about going away with Harley on a girl's trip to Thailand when she was old enough; perhaps when she finished school as a special treat. I'd been excited about the idea of sharing cocktails on the beach with her and asking her questions about her life that her mother never could. I wanted to be the '*cool Auntie*.' Now that it's all actually happening, minus the tropical location, it sickens me. It isn't right. Where is she now? I look around the silent cottage, my tongue dry with dehydration. I swallow back the little saliva I have left and taste the sour tang of wine in my mouth.

Another knock comes, sharp to my sensitive ears.

I open the door, my face ashen.

"There's a dead cat out here," a uniformed officer gestures behind him. There's a rotting stench that blows inside with the breeze.

"Doesn't look like it was a snake, looks like its neck has been crushed to me," he crouches down beside the rigid body of Jasper. Nausea hits me hard and fast. I rub at my crusty eyes, my skin feels dry and dirty against my fingertips.

"I hope I'm not disturbing; just here to do a routine check. Do you mind?" the officer on my porch steps forward away from the cat, wanting to get into the cottage. His epaulette's glisten in the sunlight. I glance at the cat, my lip curling up in disgust at the smell.

"Must've been dead for a while," the officer tells me.

"It's not mine. It's my landlords. She's been looking for him for a few days now. I'll deal with it later."

I don't want to let him in. My heart hammers so much that I'm dizzied. Black spots cloud my vision that's already in tatters. What if he finds her passed out somewhere with a hangover matching mine or worse, what if he finds her still drunk? I'd been warned someone would show up eventually to check in on how Harley was settling in with me. It had completely slipped my mind until now.

I have no choice but to open the door but all the while, I'm shaking with nerves. The fresh air makes me notice how bad the inside of my cottage smells. I've left no windows open so the space around us is heavy with sweat and alcohol. Embarrassed, I leave the front door wide open to let some fresh air in.

"Have a bit of a party last night?" he asks me, cocking an eyebrow towards the empty wine glasses and bottles scattered across the floorboards. My cheeks flourish with heat.

"Yes," I say brusquely, nodding my throbbing head. I regret it instantly. He nods, giving me a judging look. I hate him then. Surely he has a life of his own involving the occasional party. *Yes, Regan, he probably does - just not with a thirteen-year-old child.*

We walk through every room together. I'm not sure what he's looking for but I know for certain what I don't want him to find. To my pure relief, Harley is nowhere to be found.

"Is your Godchild in this morning?" he asks as we meander through her abandoned room that still gave me shivers.

"Harley!? I-uh- well," I grapple with my words, quelling the urge to pop a pain killer. I'm desperate for him to leave. It feels like my brain is imploding inside of my head.

"Can't keep up with them at this age can you?" he winks, suddenly seeming to sympathize with me.

"You have kids?" I ask him. It feels good to have what feels like a normal conversation with someone; my earlier distaste for him evaporates as he nods.

"Two daughters. Don't think they realize how much they put us through when we don't know where they are."

I guess I'm supposed to nod in response, so I do. Truthfully though, I want nothing more than Harley to stay gone. It's something I can never admit to anybody.

"How's the case going, detective?" I ask, making my way back onto the front porch with the detective hot on my heel. It's more to make conversation than anything else. I know if anything new comes up in the investigation, I'll hear about it first. Or at least, I think so. Unfortunately the reward for information on the murderer is huge and has led to hundreds of calls that have amounted to nothing. Sifting through the ever growing pile of false information regarding the night of Peyton's murder is an endless chore that I would happily take over if I was allowed to do so. It's a small town and rumors run thick especially when it concerns someone as popular as Peyton had been. *Is*. She still is popular. She always will be, even as she lay ten feet deep.

"Our resources are limited Ms. Pen, but I assure you we are doing everything possible to catch the murderer."

I eye the detective. The case hasn't gotten any further and from the dour look in his eyes, I know he doubts it ever would. It's turning cold. We share an awkward silence and the way he stares at me makes my pulse tick just that little bit faster. I wonder what he's thinking. *Guilty*. The word haunts me for no good reason. It's just my anxiety playing up again. It's time to take my pills. My pills... they seem to be controlling my life. Again. As I watch the detective walk away past Jasper who is covered in flies. His feet crunch on the gravel down the driveway. For a split second I think about not taking my pills. I think about throwing them all out.

Instead, I scrape the revolting cat up with my bare hands and take it over to the main house.

◊

My landlord is devastated but I have enough problems of my own to be dealing with hers too. I leave her sobbing at her doorway holding her dead cat in her hands and walk numbly back to the cottage.

I keep my pills, tucking them away in my bathroom cabinet and giving them one last glare before leaving the cottage. With my newly acquired child and fur baby there's a lot more shopping to do than I'm used to.

There's something about the cool, light space in the grocery store that relaxes me. I push my trolley with its broken, squeaking wheel down each aisle regardless of whether I need anything down them or not. I lose myself in the towering shelves of tins and packets for a while but I know I'll eventually wind up amongst the seemingly endless bottles of wine. I look at each label, choosing those that are most aesthetically pleasing to me. I don't care whether they're Shiraz, Merlot, Cab Sav... it's all the same to me. I used to joke that as long as there was a percentage I was happy. It's no longer a joke. The price of my box of wine turns out to be more expensive than the rest of my groceries combined; and I've chosen the cheap stuff. I can't wait to get back home and pour myself a glass. I think I'm starting to quiver and shake just from the excitement of it.

I amble back to my car in the parking lot. The bottles clang against each other noisily as the plastic handles from the bags bite into the palm of my hand. Blood pools into the tips of my fingers.

I'm busy cursing myself for parking so far away from the entrance when I hear a voice hot and heavy in my eardrum.

"Need a hand with those?"

It's the detective who had just been at my house.

"I wasn't expecting to see you again so soon!" I breathe. He's already looping his thick, dirty fingers through my shopping bags. I give them to him, trying not to blush as he looks at the six bottles of wine I refuse to let go of.

"My cars just over here," I gesture. *Stupid. He knows what car you have.*

I pop the boot and gasp. One of the carrier bags slips from my grasp and lands with a smash on the concrete. Red wine stains the floor around us. It looks like blood. My accidental drop the wine thwarts him from noticing the knife that isn't where I had left it. It's on show, gleaming in the sunlight in the center of my boot. While the detective faffs over his brown boots now splattered with my merlot, I quickly place one of the other carrier bags on top of the knife.

13

Harley is sitting at the kitchen table when I finally get back home. "Heard about Jasper? Poor little kitty," her voice drips with sarcasm. An image of Harley with her nimble little hands clasped around the cat's throat jars me momentarily. Surely not? No little girl would harm a defenseless cat.

My heart is still hammering from having such a close call with the officer in the parking lot. My mind is working too fast, thinking too many things. I slam my hand down in front of her as I release the knife. We both watch it spin on its handle for a moment.

"I thought you were taking care of it!?" I seethe. Her eyes well at the sight of it.

"Any bright ideas?" I ask, impertinent to her tears. My fingernails claw down my scalp and I grab fistfuls of hair, pulling them out by the roots. The pain feels oddly comforting. I look at myself in the window, at the wild wreck of a woman I'd seen at my parent's house. I'm getting used to her.

Her tears fall and soak the wood – that's when I scream.

"The manipulation isn't going to work!"

It takes her a moment but then she answers me, her voice so soft I have to ask her to repeat herself.

"It was all for her! I'm so scared," she rasps.

I don't know who 'her' is. I don't care. I'm electrified from the bottle of wine I'd guzzled in the car before coming inside. I'd looked at myself in the rearview mirror. I'd looked into my mother's eyes. *My eyes. I* am so scared.

"Scared of not being the center of attention anymore?!" I ask. It's the only question I already know the answer to. I just need to hear her say it.

Harley looks at me. Confused.

"No," she whispers, and walks away.

◊

I'm on the hunt for Harley's diary again the following day. I feel bad that I'm prioritizing this rather than my relationship with Craig, but I can't relax until I have answers. I also can't see Craig with the kind of hangover I'm currently battling. Even a bar tender would be bemused. Although Harley is at school, I find myself locking the front door and keeping the key dangling in the lock just to be safe. I don't want to be disturbed.

Teenagers come up with the most unoriginal hiding places. I feel it before I see it, wrapped up in one of her wooly cardigans in the cupboard. The spine cracks as I open it and I hear a gunshot from the rifle range next door. I shudder, flipping through to the latest entry. I quail at what I see. Blood smears the page. I wonder where it came from. It isn't drawn in any kind of particular pattern. No words are formed. It's just blots of blood on paper, making the page crinkly and stiff. I wonder briefly if it could be the cats, but I didn't notice any blood on his body when I'd picked him up.

At the top of the page written in terrible handwriting is yesterday's date.

I don't understand! I did it all for her! WHY can't Regan see that???

That's it. Vague.

"Give me more!" I bellow, shaking her stupid book in my hands. The cat startles and hisses at me unappreciatively.

I slip a bottle of vodka into my handbag. I've always hated the stuff. Mum used to drink it when she started hiding her drinking from us. It was the only booze that didn't smell of anything. I don't know why I'm drinking more and more of it these days. I never actively hide my drinking. Do I?

Peyton's tombstone is scattered with an array of flowers. I find myself laughing at the fake bouquets, both cheap but sensible. I guess they make more sense. They'd last longer.

I kneel in front of her. *Probably on top of her.* The thought makes me shiver. I chuck a shot of vodka over her grave, wetting the grass that has already grown above her. I know she'd appreciate the sentiment. I toast to her. Raising the entire bottle of vodka to her name etched in stone, I drain its contents. My throat burns and I choke but don't stop until every last drop is down my gullet. *Atta girl*, I can hear Peyton say. I smile with her.

I stay with her for hours, watching other mourners shuffle around the graves trying to locate their loved ones. There should be a map for these kinds of places, or maybe they do have them in other graveyards. Just not in a tiny town like ours.

I speak to Peyton as if she can actually hear me. I ask her again and again what Harley meant when she said she'd done it for 'her'. I ask her who 'her' is. I ask if it's her way of confessing, but even if it is I can already feel the words she said starting to slip away from my grasp. It's like Harley's sentence is melting in my mind. I remember her words, but struggle to put them together. I can't place her voice and those words together properly.

Had she really said them? My uncertainty terrifies me. What is going on with my mind? Why can't I focus? I take a sip from another bottle, and another.

I have her journal as proof. I've taken a photo of the page with my phone. I unlock the screen and scroll through my gallery. My breath catches. It's not there.

I check three times but the photo I'd taken crouched over the pages of Harley's journal is gone. I had taken it. I know I had.

I rack my brain, go over the evening I had caught her with Sean. I had seen that. It was real… wasn't it? I take a sip, and another. Lock and unlock my phone. Check my gallery again. Nothing. I click onto my messages and see the little round photographs of all of the people I have been in recent contact with. There aren't many. Sean is still there but he is still blocked. I open up our conversation. Click unblock. His profile photo fades and reappears instantly as something new. My stomach clenches. I know even before I expand the image that it's a photograph of him and *her*. She's kissing his cheek. They're sitting next to a blazing fireplace. There's a dog in his arms, red wine and beer cans on a cloth covered table. They look happy. It hurts.

I think about all of the times I begged him to change his profile picture to one of us after I found out he cheated. I wanted him to show everyone that he was taken so that the women he used to text dirty things to behind my back wouldn't text him back. I wanted to eliminate all possibilities of him cheating again. It had caused so many fights. He'd refused to update his profile picture, told me I was being silly and petty. He was still texting those other women, even if I could no longer prove it.

He hadn't changed his picture for me, but he did for her. I look at her. One of the eight women he'd strung along behind my back, but she was always different. She was always more. I'd found out about her last, but she'd been around for the longest. What does she have that I don't? I measure myself up against her in absolutely every way because she is better than me. I just want to understand why? How had she changed him? She has, hasn't she? If he has given up his 'freedom' and is so happy to show the world he's with her now then surely he didn't sleep with Harley. I'd imagined it. I squeeze my eyes shut and bite at my nails, trying to remember something that never even happened. *No*. It *did* happen. I have to believe it. I have to trust myself.

I look at the photograph of Sean and his new girlfriend. I want to message her and tell her how stupid she is. I want to tell her about his ways.

Leave them alone... a voice in my head reasons. I finish the second bottle.

I look at the grin on his face, at his eyes so blue they hurt to look at. He has changed for her. My heart breaks, not for him, but for myself. For not being good enough for him. I block him again, knowing it would be the advice Peyton would give me if she were here.

Let it go.

I'm not expecting Craig to come when he texts to ask where I am. But he does. I hear his shoes crunching on parched stems of grass, dust getting kicked up behind him. He crouches down beside me and doesn't say a thing. He looks at the empty bottles by my knees, sighs and cradles me.

I don't say it, but in my mind I'm wondering where he came from. This incredible man, so sweet and affectionate; goofy, loving and understanding... so unlike anyone I have ever encountered before. I wouldn't say I'm a bad person, yet I still ask myself what I did to deserve someone like him. Instead of questioning him, us, I thank him, my voice a whisper in the wind. I can be happy, too. I can make this work with Craig. I need it.

"I'm not going anywhere," he says, simply. I nod. For once, I believe those words.

"Baby, I need you to stop drinking so much."

His words sting, embarrassing me only because I know it's true. My shoulders begin to shake and tears well in my eyes as I nod, again. I look up at him and make a silent promise that I'll try. He walks me back to my car, tossing the empty vodka bottles into a bin swarming with flies.

◊

Harley steps into the kitchen, padding over to the kettle and flicking it on. She's drowning in a jumper she doesn't need in this weather. I'm in a good mood after spending just that small amount of time with Craig earlier; it's like he'd revitalized me. I hate knowing that right now I am reliant on a man, like he's the pinnacle point to my sanity. I never wanted to be that woman, but he is helping me through something I can't do alone at this stage.

Harley stands on tip toes, craning her neck into the cupboard above the kettle to find the box of tea. She's still too short to reach properly.

"What's that?" I blurt before I have a chance to think. I've just caught a glimpse of something on her arms. My first thought is that she's gone and tattooed herself. The detective will love that.

"Nothing," she says, too quickly. She pulls at the baggy sleeves, clutching onto them with her fingernails. Onions sizzle angrily in boiling oil.

"Harley," I say, sternly. I'm sober now, for once, and I'm not going to let this slide.

"Just leave me alone, alright?!"

I walk over to her, feeling steadier on my feet than normal but I notice my hands starting to tremble. I don't want to believe it's from the lack of drinking.

She tries to leave the room but I corner her, gripping her arm firmly and pulling up the sleeve of her left arm. I feel instantly sick. Infected, inflamed letters gorge her once flawless tan skin, trailing all the way up her forearm. I tug at the zip of her jumper and tear the clothing from her. She's no longer fighting me, instead she shrugs it off in defeat.

"Regan, please," she begs and sobs. The mutilation goes all the way up to her shoulder.

All of the letters were H's.

My hand flies to my mouth in horror; the blood in her journal. It's hers. She's been cutting herself. Carving her name into her skin.

"You're sick!" I cry.

"Are you really this shallow that you actually want to engrave your own initials into your skin!?"

She looks taken aback and breathes hard.

"It's not my initials. The H's stand for Help!" she screams, her little chest heaving.

The smell of burning onions drifts to my nostrils.

*

I never had anybody when I was cutting myself. Nobody noticed. Nobody cared. Doesn't make for the ideal person to take care of a situation like this. To be honest, even if someone had seen what I was doing to myself, I don't know what I would have wanted them to say or do. I don't even know how I got better. Did I ever get better? I think it went from the cutting straight to the drinking. What a step up.

The point is, one day I just stopped. I remember it, though. I remember being in a shoebox of an apartment, the bedroom the only room in the place beside the bathroom with a shower I had to bend my knees to fit under. I'd been drinking and was a wreck, sniveling into my sleeves and looking at myself in the bathroom mirror. My problems weren't as bad as I liked to let myself believe, there were so many others out there with far worse worries than me. I think that's one of the reasons I resented myself, my reflection. I was selfish. While there were people out there with real problems here I was crying myself to sleep with a bandaged wrist and a hangover waiting to wake me up. Over what? Being cheated on and an alcoholic family? That was the extent of my problems back then. To me though, it was enough to push me over the edge and I couldn't fight it. I let it win. I let it take me over.

My scars prickle and tingle beneath my cardigan now. I hate the expression, but I am lost for words.

It's only much later when I realized there were a lot of smaller scratches covering her arms amongst the letters she'd carved into her skin. Cat scratches.

14

Harley doesn't given me a chance to respond. She flees the cottage, her sweet perfume following after her. I call my dad. I can't tell him what I've seen over the phone. I can't get the words out.

"Can I come over?" I ask, once again feeling that strange unfamiliar feeling of reliance.

"You know you're always more than welcome, darling. Mum isn't good though," he warns.

When is she ever good? I want to ask. The warning doesn't surprise me at all. I bite my tongue and sling my bag over one shoulder.

Dad pours me a glass of white wine, it brims the edge of the glass. I don't want it, but I take it because I need it. I bring the glass to my lips and exhale with relief at the mere smell of it.

It's a smell I love.

It's a smell I hate.

It's a smell I can't resist.

"Where's mum?" I ask as I plant myself into one of the cracked red leather chairs we've had since before I was born.

"Bed," he rolls his eyes, twirling a tumbler filled with amber liquid around in his hand.

I look at the clock, 6pm, a reasonable enough hour to have a drink, but not to be sleeping.

"She needs a hobby or a job to keep her busy, dad," I say. I need one too, everyone in this family does. I keep my thoughts to myself.

"She needs rehab," he says back.

I look up sharply.

"Then send her?"

"I've tried, darling!" his voice raises an octave in defense. He's agitated, knocking back the last of his drink before refilling.

"What do you mean you've tried?"

"Rehab is a voluntary thing. If she doesn't want to go, I can't make her... and even if we got to that stage they wouldn't take her anyway. She needs to go to hospital first to detox."

I don't know if he's telling me the truth or not. I don't care. It feels good to be focusing on something other than Harley. He sets his tumbler down in front of him, clumsily. *When had things become so bad in this family?*

"Surely there's something we can do?"

"How's Harley?" he asks, licking whiskey from his lips. He isn't looking at me. He's looking at the floor as if ashamed to meet my eyes.

"Can never escape her for long," I mutter under my breath. Dad's head tilts questioningly.

I shake my head, tip more wine into my mouth. I eye his pack of cigarettes on the coffee table.

"She's cutting herself," I allow myself to admit finally. Now I can't look at him either. I know he knows I used to cut myself. He just found out too late... and after he knew, it was too late to do anything about it. I'd already stopped.

"Is it bad?"

"It's awful. She's going to be scarred for life, all up her left arm. She's so angry," I choke.

Dad rearranges himself, plucking a cigarette from the carton. It has a picture of a tiny baby, its skull tiny and delicate. It has breathing tubes up its nose, taped across its face. It. From the picture it's impossible to tell if it's a boy or a girl. It doesn't matter. It never matters. I take a cigarette too, turning the box over out of sight and click the lighter.

"Dad," I whisper. Whimper.

He looks at me, waiting. I need to tell him. I need him to listen, to believe me.

"Dad, Harley had something to do with Peyton's murder. I know it!" He's already turning away from me before I've even finished my sentence. I carry on blabbering, telling him about the knife in her room covered in blood and how she was with Sean, seducing the men in my life.

"Regan, stop this nonsense!" he slams his hand down, knocking over both of our drinks. Recognition of the violent man he used to be hits me. His aggression shocks me. He's been a gentle giant for so many years now.

"You. Need. To. Stop!" he says, slowly. His tone is harsh. Unforgiving.

"But dad, I-."

"No! Regan, the police are doing everything they can. If she had something to do with it they would have found that out by now. You're being dramatic and stupid!" his words puncture through the last bit of my strength. I can't stand that he can see how much he'd hurt me.

"Why are you getting so angry?" I demand, my eyes burning with tears.

My mother staggers into the room and we both look up at her. My jaw drops. Deep purple bruises bulge beneath her eyes.

◊

"What happened to you?" I can't hide the disgust in my face. I can barely recognize her. Her hair looks like it hasn't been brushed in weeks; there's a bald patch showing at the top of her head. As her feet drag her into the room and she looms closer, I can see that her face is caked in makeup too pale for her skin-tone, it does nothing to cover up the bruises.

It's only when she's standing right above me, too close to me, that she smiles.

"Hiya," she slurs, looking between my father and I; at the glasses on the floor.

"Oh no. What happened? Let me get you both topped up," she smiles at us with discolored teeth, her lips quivering the way mine had earlier. No.

She turns towards the bar and I notice that she has a large urine patch across the back of her sweatpants.

"Oh fuck. You've wet the bed again, haven't you?" my dad bellows accusingly, jumping to his feet. I'm startled but my mother doesn't seem to notice anything that's going on around her. Instead of topping up our glasses, she reaches for a new one in the cabinet and pours herself a drink.

"You don't need another one!" dad yells. She carries on pouring with a smirk on her face. This is why I couldn't live at home... yet it seems things have gotten worse since I left. I close my eyes, breathing in deeply. The room has become fragrant with my mother's body odor.

"What's happening?" mum asks, positioning herself between us with her glass clasped in both hands. Our glasses still lay on the floor.

"I was trying to talk to dad about Harley. I think she has something to do with Peyton's death," I say, searching my mother's emotionless eyes for anything. Nothing.

"Well, I-" mum begins, but dad cuts her off.

"Sweetie, you need to go and have a shower." His voice is still hard.

He's always called her sweetie, even during their worst arguments.

Mum stares into her glass, this frail woman who had once been so

strong and independent. She had once been my role-model. Look at

her now.

"Harley is-" she starts.

"Now!" dad's voice booms across the room making both me and my

mother recoil.

Why is he cutting her off? Why doesn't he want her to speak? Is he

protecting her? I think back to my theory that my mother could

have had something to do with the murder. I want to laugh. *Look at

her...*

But she is mad... I remind myself.

My mother's jaw juts forward as she spins on her heels and leaves

the room. I'm once again left alone with my father. He unlaces his

fingers and stares at me as though we're in solidarity over how he

had treated my mother, yet I feel oddly sorry for her amidst the

resentment. I'm overcome by the intense feeling that I'm missing

something.

When Harley texts to find out where I am (not that I actually think

she cares, she only really wants to know what's for dinner), I ignore

her. I curl up on the sofa in my father's sitting room, wrapping myself in the knitted blanket that usually drapes over the armrest. A candle on the table next to me flickers; it smells of chili spice and cinnamon.

The home phone chimes in another room but before I can tell them not to answer it, my mother picks up the receiver.

"Harley!" I hear her voice instantly brighten. She invites her over for a dinner that hasn't been prepared. We settle on ordering in a couple of pizzas as mum as always is too drunk to cook and dad has had enough. Even with my irritation at Harley's arrival, I can't help but be ashamed of my family.

Mum's made an effort. She's put herself through the shower and tugged what remains of her hair into a bun on top of her balding scalp. She's changed, dumping her piss drenched sweats into the laundry for another day. Her Angel perfume wafts from her neck and bosom, but it still isn't enough to hide the stench of alcohol. *She's trying...* I keep telling myself.

Harley's wearing a dress fresh out of my wardrobe. I bite back the desire to tear it right from her body. It's a silky, full length cocktail dress with sleeves that ravel up by her wrists. Her knickers-line is clearly visible at the rear and she's paired it with a pair of dirty converse lace-ups. It gives me more satisfaction than it should that my feet are far bigger than hers. For now my shoes belong solely to me.

My parents don't ask her about the dress or what's beneath it, throbbing and pulsing through her left arm. I however, can almost smell the infected skin. She doesn't look well either. It isn't just that the light green dress looks terrible against her skin tone, she has dark rings under her eyes and she seems pale despite her dark complexion. Her collarbone stands out to a sickening degree and her skinniness makes me nauseous. Her hips and bust are starting to develop and her bottom is full and round, but everything else about her is too small. It doesn't match her frame.

She spears cherry tomatoes and plops them into her mouth, refusing to touch any other part of the pizza. My irritation is rapidly building.

My phone rings loudly, breaking the awkward silence circulating the room.

"I'll just-" I gesture to my phone, leaping out of my seat and escaping the dinner table.

I stare as Sean's name flashes up on the screen, unsure what to do. Blocking him from messaging me was easy enough but without me being exactly tech savvy, I didn't know how to block him from calling. I guess I could have Googled it. I guess I was too lazy and now it's too late.

The truth is that I haven't been expecting him to call. His photograph fills every corner of the screen, his blue eyes piercing and bright. He looks like a young Mel Gibson. His skin too tanned, his body too stocky, his eyes too blue. He has that same smug look, too. I can't believe I used to find Mel Gibson attractive. I can't believe I used to find *Sean* attractive. He ss the filthiest looking man in the world to me now.

I swallow my hate and swipe to answer.

I stand there in silence, hearing nothing but the sound of his breathing for a few seconds. When his voice does come through he sounds confused.

"Hello, you there?" he says. Even in his forties, he still sounds like his voice is breaking sometimes. I remain still and silent, aware that I can't even breathe. Why is he calling me?

"Look, Regan... I know you're there. Just... call me. I'm here for a month and I think we should talk..." his voice trails off. My nostrils flare and my lip curls. I want to scream at him and ask him how dare he call me. I want to cry and ask him why. I want to ask him about Harley; I'm still not sure if I'd imagined it or not.

I never want to see him again but I want him to see me and see what he's lost. I want everything and I want nothing.

I hang up and draw in a breath. When I exhale, I notice that I'm shaking again.

I wonder into dad's lounge and pour a glass of whiskey over some ice, knowing that Sean will call me again.

◊

I down the drink and sit in silence until my electrified nerves calm. I hate the effect Sean has on me. I hate the effect booze has on me. When I return to my family, I find my mother holding Harley. They are both crying. Dad is nowhere to be seen. They look so close, too close. Jealousy courses through me. Why are they crying? How had they become so close? Had Harley opened up to her about her cuts? Although these endless questions whirl through my brain, I don't care for the answers. I'm across the room, whiskey hot on my breath as I huff, pulling Harley from my mother's embrace. My body feels light and free, warm from the tumbler of dad's booze.

"We're going," I say, shoving Harley towards the front door. My mother doesn't try to stop us, just sits there rubbing her eyes with scrunched up fists.

We leave without as much as a goodbye.

"You're absolutely crazy!" Harley yells out of the blue as I drive well above the speed limit. Maybe I am crazy.

I want to tell her that I won't allow her to steal my parents, but I see no point. Instead I choose to warn her with the one thing I think she might understand.

"Do *not* get your hopes up with those two. They are not the kind of people you go to when you need help, Harley. They have more than enough issues of their own."

Nightmares haunt me that night. Years of being let down by my parents come hurtling towards me in horrifyingly vivid dreams, but one wakes me up in a cold sweat. It takes me a moment to steady my breathing and lower my heart-rate, to make sure I'm not back there. It was a dream but it was a memory, too. A memory from the first time I'd fought back against my father. He'd been drunk and aggressive, shouting so loud that I wasn't sure how the neighbors could simply ignore us.

I remember trying to leave the house, get away from it all. He was smashing anything he could get hold of in the house, shoving my mother around. I opened the front door only to see a hand fly past my face and splinter the wood from the doorframe as it slammed. I remember being tugged back into the house so hard, I grabbed his shirt for support and before I knew what I was doing... I kicked. I got him right in the groin and he fell. I took it as my chance to run but I wasn't quick enough. Before I'd even made it halfway across the room, he tackled me, ramming me over so that I tumbled over the sofa. I fought back, pushing, kicking against my own father who had such brittle bones but I didn't care then if I broke some of them... I didn't even care if I killed him in that moment... but I wasn't strong enough. He hurtled me into a glass coffee table – I've never had bruises like that in my life. Not even from Sean. I remember the strength it took for me to get up, while he was still squirming around on the coffee table in his drunken state. I darted out of the room and tried to escape through the back door, all the while hatred seeping into me because my own mother had just stood and stared as my dad did that to me. The back door was locked and by the time I'd realized that dad was up again, I ran into the kitchen but he pushed me and I fell over a bicycle. When I was able to push him off of me and stand, I screamed at the top of my lungs and told him I wished he was dead. He'd just recovered from tuberculosis and had been supposed to die, it was a miracle he was still alive. My words cut him at the core and he froze, letting me go. I remember that feeling of running barefoot through the streets along the lagoon road trying to get away, the salty breeze whipping my face. The one thing that hadn't been a memory were the screams I'd heard in the dream from my mother. She was screaming, "help her!" Her screams were continuous and earsplitting, so when her voice morphed into Peyton's I barely noticed... but then Peyton's sobbing face appeared and everything else fell away.

"I'm so sorry. Please, help her, Regan," she begged.

I wake with a jolt. I've never had such a vivid dream. I've never really been much of a dreamer but lately they won't stop. I sit up in bed, slowly piecing together the dream in the darkness. I can still hear my mother screaming, Peyton begging and the sound of my bare feet slapping again the concrete road as I ran away from it all. I often feel like that now... like I'm on some dark, forlorn road running away from everything.

I open up Facebook and scroll through my newsfeed. It doesn't even shock me anymore when I see yet another friend changing her status to 'engaged' or their partner posting some sickening update about how 'she said yes!'

Oh, Tia just got pregnant. What a shocker.

Kate's off on her honeymoon to catch mahi-mahi in Mauritius.

Sammi's perched up against a windowsill overlooking the ocean on a romantic date night.

Post after post, it's always something similar. If it isn't something loved up like that it's posting photographs or ridiculous updates about children.

'It was their first day of school today! Look how cute they look in their outfits!' or, 'Kacy decided to use the Big Girl potty for the first time today! Growing up way too fast!'

I want to vomit. I also find myself, for the first time ever, feeling really envious. I want that too.

I think that's why I've been so distant with all of the other friends I had here since I've been back. I feel like I'm on such a different level to them. The day I'd seen them all at Peyton's house they all had these big rocks glittering on their fingers or bulging stomachs or wedding plans they couldn't shut up about. I just can't relate. I feel so far apart from all of them.

I want what they have.

I text Craig.

Come over x

15

We're in bed together, both catching our breaths after multiple orgasms. The Big Five before nine AM, he jokes.

I lay draped over him, my face against his hairy chest that seems more like a fluffy blanket. He's drawing circles with his fingers onto my shoulder blades.

"If you were reincarnated, what would you be?" I ask him, my voice muffled. I smile as I feel him shift, considering his options.

"A sperm whale," he finally decides. I laugh into him, smelling our sweat and sex against his skin.

"You already are one," I say, smacking him playfully and nuzzling myself deeper into him.

It's there, in that moment, that everything in the world feels OK. Things finally feel right. It's a strange moment when it hits you. I'd never really had that feeling with Sean although I guess I tried to think I had. With Craig, I feel like I'm on the right track; that this is it... and I find myself thinking about the future in a way I never actually had with Sean. I'm thinking about marriage and what our kids would look like and how if that ever did happen I would make sure this new family I was creating would be the furthest thing from the family I currently have.

I don't know why I feel like I want to share the feeling aloud.

"Craig, can I tell you something?" I say, smiling. Something about this all feels so good, so right.

"Anything," he shifts so he can look down at me. I breathe him in.

"I think you're it for me. I feel it, you know?"

I'm certain I feel him freeze.

"Wow, Regan. That's... that's really sweet of you to say."

I start to panic. I start blurting things out at lightning speed.

"I can't imagine being with anyone else but you. I don't want to be with anyone else but you ever again, you know? I see a future with you. I can imagine things with you that I never have with anyone. I mean, can you imagine how gorgeous our babies would be?"

Now I definitely feel him freeze.

I'm suddenly desperate, wanting him to tell me that he wants all of that with me too. All of my girlfriends have it, why couldn't I have it too? It is making me crazy.

"That sounds amazing, Ray," he says now, stroking my hair and pulling me into his chest again. Ray. His ray of sunshine. Not the most unique name I've heard but coming from him it feels different. Special.

"Really?" I play with his chest hair and the oils from his skin. I feel his sigh.

"Yes. But I'd like to focus on us having fun and enjoying each other. Is that OK?"

My heart drops but I nod anyway. Yes, yes it's OK, I tell him. I lie.

"But for the record, yes... I do think they'd be pretty damn good looking children," his kisses perk me up.

When he disentangles himself from me, rolling out of bed and heads to the bathroom, I can't help but stare gleefully at his ass. Tufts of dark hair cover both cheeks but on him I find it sexy.

As soon as the door to the bathroom closes, my mood wavers. What if he isn't sure about me? I feel sick at the thought.

What if there's a reason he doesn't want to get serious?

There's an old adage that goes, *'What you don't know won't hurt you.'*

I've never listened to bits of wisdom like that. Sometimes, I wish I did.

I don't know what makes me do it. Something is growing inside of me, a sense of unease. Things are too perfect and something has to go wrong. I'm questioning him for no apparent reason other than wanting to protect myself.

By now I know his patterns. He'd always shower after sex, coming back a good ten minutes later smelling fresh and so irresistible he just get dirty all over again if I had my way with him. Knowing I have those ten minutes, I drag myself across the bed, propping myself up on his pillow. His phone is flashing with unread messages and my heart thumps. I click the button at the bottom of the phone and enter his passcode. He's done it in front of me so many times that

I've been able to memorize it. I keep trying to tell myself that with him being so open about his passwords means there couldn't possibly be anything on his phone to hide, that he wouldn't do what Sean did to me. I wish I could believe myself. Sometimes I do, but more often than not I can't.

Nerves and adrenalin rush through me as I tap into his messages, trawling through his phone. I scroll through. Most of the texts are from me. Others are from his mother, asking him if he'd remembered to feed her fish. She's away traveling in Egypt and was filling him in on her mid-life crisis adventure. He has others from staff at the bar either bailing on their shifts or asking him for advice; nothing from girls. I won't say its disappointment I feel, but it's something strange. I'm so used to being cheated on and lied to. A part of me was sure there would be something there to break us up. There had to be... but there wasn't.

I click into his gallery and find nothing but a bunch of silly memes and a folder filled with images of damages at the bar. No nudes, no girls, nothing. I feel deflated only because I've worked myself up into believing this would be the moment it would all fall apart. I'd find something and be able to run away before he was able to really hurt me the way Sean had done. But there's nothing.

I click into his Facebook page, hating myself for the invasion of privacy but desperate to find something. Anything. I know if I do find something I will hate it but if I don't look, I could be getting lied to. I'm not proud of my snooping and I wish I could say this would be a once off – but I can't. Sean has turned me into a paranoid wreck of a woman, convinced that there are no good men in the world. Not now, not ever. His messages on Facebook come up clean. The last message he's received on there is from over a year ago. Clearly he doesn't use the app very often. I hear the shower nozzle turn off and the sound of the towel getting tugged from the railing. With time running out I realized I have nothing. I should be satisfied but a part of me is certain if I looked hard enough, I'd find something. Anything.

I click on the Search icon at the top and see a list of his most recently searched and viewed profiles on Facebook. All of them are women. I'm on the list. Not at the top, quite far down actually, wedged between a Diana and a Lucy... but what irks me the most isn't that. What gets me is that the last profile Craig had pulled up, the last person he's looked up... is Harley.

I stare dumbly at the screen, my ears ringing, my vision blurring. Craig is humming now, something he always does just before opening the bathroom door. It usually makes me laugh, him and his terrible singing, but now I'm frozen. Silent.

I lock his screen, hoping I place the phone back where he'd left it. He comes out and smiles down at me, buoyed-up from sex and a shower. I feel so small, huddled in a ball under his bed-sheets.

Vulnerable. It's a feeling I never wanted again.

I want to ask him what he was doing stalking Harley on Facebook.

I'm not certain if I'm more concerned about that or feeling more

possessive over Craig, remembering how she had seduced Sean.

Craig isn't like Sean...

That's what you always think... You're always wrong, Regan.

I can't – I won't listen to myself. I need to stop my thoughts. My

head is spinning out of control. Forcing a smile took all of my effort.

Now I know why they say it uses more muscles than frowning.

Suddenly too aware of my body, I wrap the sheets around me and

fly towards the bathroom. Craig's chuckles follow behind me as I

turn the shower on.

"When did you become so shy?" he asks. He's standing so close to

me I can feel the warmth of his breath prickle the back of my neck.

My hair is scooped up into a bun. He pulls it loose. My hair falls

around my shoulders and my skin explodes in goose bumps.

His fingers brush carefully down my curves, making my neck twist;

my body responding to his touch. His mouth draws up to my ear,

nipping and sucking at my lobe the way he knows I like it. My

breathing quickens, growing heavy as I close my eyes. I want

desperately to enjoy it, but I can't stop thinking of Harley. First

Harley with Sean – but then the vivid images in my head change to

Harley and Craig. Together.

"Stop!" I say, pulling away. He's hard against my backside.

"Regan?"

I step beneath the tepid spray of water, unable to look at him. I feel unhinged from reality... the familiar feeling of dread that my boyfriend is doing something awful completely taking hold of me. "Not right now," I manage to whisper, the chasm between how we had been earlier to now growing. I don't know if he hears me or not over the sound of the shower but I turn around when the bathroom door clicks shut on his way out. I stand there for ages, washing him off of me. *Pedophile*... the word hits me so hard I think I might be sick.

◊

"Harley, find the knife!"

I've been turning the cottage upside down ever since getting home. It's gone. Harley walks into my bedroom and sees me on hands and knees looking under the bed. I don't know where she's been. I don't care.

She's unperturbed by my frenzy.

"I've taken care of it," she says flippantly.

"Give me the knife, right now," I chivvy.

"I don't know what you're so worried about. Everything's going to be OK now," she says, glossing over the situation.

I'm trying to find something else to focus on, not wanting to believe Harley has caught Craig's attention in any way, shape or form. So I hold onto the fact that the knife isn't where I left it, forcing the thought of Harley with Craig as far from my mind as I possibly can.

"Your secret's safe with me," she says, standing over me now. There's a chuckle in her voice. I look up at her, exhaustion seeping through me.

"What secret?" I ask as she walks away. She turns then, looking at me as though I'm crazy. I'm starting to think that I am.

"WHY do you keep pretending you don't know?!" her chest billows as she breathes in deeply, exasperated. It feels as though something is being left unsaid.

"Because I don't want to believe it's true!"

"It's true," Harley says simply, throwing me a sinister look that I don't understand. I don't understand anything anymore. Everything is too cryptic, too confusing.

"How can you say that with a smile on your face? Do you really have no heart?"

"Heart?! Everything was for her!" her voice is a high-pitched squeal now. The cat leaps from my bed and darts from the room in fury, hair standing on end. Miserable bastard. Even he has had enough of the two of us.

Everything was for her… the same words from her diary. The same words I wasn't sure if she'd really said or not. Here they are, formed from her lips. I don't understand what they mean.

There's a bottle of wine I'd stashed in the telescope that stands beside my thighs now. I had been just about to take a swig when I heard her come home. I'd promised Craig I'd try and I wanted to. In fact, I challenged myself to stay away from the bottle. I kept glancing at the clock to see how many hours it had been. I'd made green tea with ginger slices and I had felt good about it – but I could still hear the clock ticking in the back of my head. Plaguing me.

Harley looks at the bottle as though she's only just noticed it, a look of pity on her face. I feel so small, seeing myself through her eyes. She kicks it, sending it skittering across the floorboards.

"You really are crazy," I hang my head low, shaking.

I feel fingers on my face. She grips my chin and tips my face up to look at her.

"Don't *ever* say that again," her voice is hoarse and with that, her open palm slams against my cheek. I hear a crack and taste blood, my ears whirring.

I trace the fingerprints emblazoned on my face and despite everything, I laugh. It is uncontrollable, a deep belly laugh making my shoulders shake. It's the same kind of inappropriate laughter I always get at the worst of times, when I can't believe what's going on around me. I don't believe it now.

I crawl into my bathroom, wine bottle in hand, and punch two pills from a packet. I draw the curtains shut as I hoist myself up, ready to swallow them with some wine. Dust particles fall like tiny snowflakes all around me, around the framed photograph of a time when Peyton was still alive. I watch her as the wine pours from the bottle into my mouth. I lick my lips, already stained red.

When I calm down I try to call my mother. I haven't needed her for so long but suddenly I miss her. I miss her something terrible, even though I see her all the time... but then, that's not really her. I want to talk to her, tell her my problems. I want to listen to her problems. But she doesn't answer. Instead, I leave a voicemail, my voice uncertain as I tell her I need her. I love her. I try Craig next but the ringing stops abruptly. I know he's hung up on me. I want to believe he's done it because he's in a meeting or he's busy driving, but I know he's upset with me. It feels like everyone is avoiding me. Even Sean has stopped calling, his persistence dwindling with his boredom.

When had everyone given up on me? They'd all tried so hard to be there for me. My parents inviting me over for dinner, wanting me to stay with them, Craig being so patient and kind, even Sean with his phone calls. I had people around and I'd managed to push them all away. Even Harley. We were finally getting along. Now I am alone with nothing but a packet of anxiety medication and a bottle of wine, a moaning, paranoid, wreck that has become one of those girls who go through their boyfriends phones. Even to myself I sound pathetic. Self-absorbed.

"You're so hard on yourself," Craig had whispered after sex just that morning when I lay on my stomach telling him about my failings with Harley. He'd been tickling my back, running his long fingers through my hair. It had felt so good, so relaxing. I'd do anything to go back there now, to not have looked at his phone... but I can't take it back and now I'm going to have to ask him before it eats me alive. He has to have a good explanation. He has to.

With the pills slowly calming me down and grounding me, I call out to Harley.

"I'm out for the night. You can't stay here alone. I'll be waiting in the car to drive you to my folks place," I say. I need to go to Craig. I need to explain myself and why I had acted so strangely.

After five minutes I toot the horn, refusing to go back inside to drag Harley out. She sticks her head out of her bedroom window.

"I'm old enough to stay in alone, you know!" she tells me. She fixes me with an annoyed look that only an immature teenager uses.

"You're still a child," I say. I'm in a bitchy mood. Riled up. Ready to go.

Her jaw drops.

"Why don't you want to go to my precious parent's house anyway? You seem to have bonded with my mother so nicely."

"You don't know what the fuck you're talking about!" she yells, her dark eyes looking over at the pathway to the landlords house.

I giggle, not sure if it was from the pills not taking full effect yet or because they had. Her little lips uttering swear words seemed hysterical to me.

"You need help..." Harley says, shutting her window and leaving me alone in my car with nothing but the sound of my own laughter.

16

I hear the blow of a rifle as I reverse out of the driveway. It makes me jump in my car seat. I'll never get used to that.

Craig isn't at home when I get to his place. My excitement to see him and to explain myself abates as I see his empty parking space. I head to his bar, running over what I'm going to say to him in my head. I'm vaguely aware that I'm grinding my teeth.

The door opens with a creak and oscillates back and forth as I step inside.

"Craig?" The bar is empty, cold. My feet echoing across the floorboards that have an always present scent of beer.

"In here," he calls back. I follow the sound of his voice into a freezer room. I wrap my arms around myself and catch him putting chilled white wines into a cardboard box.

"Restocking," he explains briefly. He's short with me, busy. Perhaps not the most auspicious moment to be discussing why I was acting so weird earlier. I start to wonder if I should have waited longer, let things cool off. It was our first argument, if you can even call it that.

"Look, I always do this. I find a reason to mess things up. I've always done it. Whenever my feelings start to grow, I do something to ruin things. I guess it's my way of protecting myself because whenever I have feelings for someone I always end up getting hurt."

My words are pouring out of my mouth, forming themselves with no thought or help from me.

He's looking at me strangely, the way everyone looks at me lately. I sigh.

"I looked at your phone," I admit, not wanting to meet his eyes. Shame floods me. When I peek up, I see that his eyes have darkened; his mouth a firm line.

"Get out," he says. The anger I'd expected to see in his eyes to match his tone of voice wasn't there, instead he was looking at me with disappointment. That made things worse.

"What?" I feel my knees buckle. He's kicking me out.

Oops I did it again, Britney. I mucked up another relationship with my fear of getting hurt.

"You went into my phone, Regan. You invaded my privacy. It's not like you'd find anything there anyway, I'm an open book!' his hands are flapping.

I feel reprimanded, weak and vulnerable. Then I remember how he'd searched for Harley on Facebook.

"Harley!" I cry above the roaring sound of the fans around us, chugging icy air around the sealed room. The salient point of why I am here gives me courage. I'm here to demand an explanation so that we can move on. I want to hear what he has to say. I *need* to hear what he has to say.

"Excuse me?" Craig says, his voice is a growl.

He lifts up a cardboard box and places it on a stool. He can't keep still. When he's placed the box down he strides towards me, invading my personal space like I invaded his. He is too close to me; I can smell garlic on his breath. I see a vein pulsing in his temple and his biceps throbbing.

It suddenly dawns on me that if he was to do something to me here in this freezer room, no one would hear me.

"You looked Harley up – on Facebook," I falter. Even to myself I sound ridiculous.

Craig exhales and for a moment I think he is going to punch the stainless steel wall. His fist is so tightly balled up that his knuckles turn white.

I close my eyes, bracing myself... and I open them with a start as I hear the slam of the door.

He's walked out and locked me in here.

Fear drenches me in a cold sweat and I scream. I scream so loudly that I don't recognize the noises I make.

I rush to the door and bang loudly. Someone has to be able to hear me.

"Regan, what the hell?!" Craig shouts as I fall forward. He's opened the door. I consider running, feeling like I'm in some sort of thriller movie where the woman only has one chance to escape.

I scramble to my feet.

"You locked me in," I stammer.

"What!? There's a handle on the door," he says, gesturing towards a handle with a sign in vinyl above is reading, 'PUSH'.

How had I missed that?

We stand there and look at one another in absolute silence. I feel like he's looking at me for the first time. I feel like he doesn't like what he sees. I wonder if he's thinking to himself, *this is why Sean left this crazy bitch!*

Whatever I'm expecting, it isn't his laughter. It isn't the kind of laughter that makes it sound like he's found something funny. It's the kind of laughter that sounds tired. He rubs his eyes and leans his head against the door.

"I wouldn't lock you in the freezer you idiot," he says. There's affection in his voice.

"But-".

"No buts. I'm a good guy Regan. I would never hurt you and there really wasn't any need to look at my phone. You are the only woman I wanted."

Wanted. Past tense. My stomach lurches. So it is over.

"*Still* want," he clarifies as though reading my mind. He picks my hands up with his. I look him in eyes, tears rolling down my cheeks. I don't know what to say.

"Now what's this about Harley?" he asks me. He sounds so soft and patient that it makes me feel terrible for ever having doubted him.

"You looked her up on Facebook," I mumble. *I think you're a pedophile*, I think.

"To find something she's interested in, Regan! To be able to start a conversation with her at the dinner table and make an effort," he says. His hands are on my arms, rubbing them vigorously in an attempt to warm me up. He's so caring, so innocuous.

My heart breaks as I realize what I've accused him of. In that moment, despite how wonderful he's being, I'm convinced we'll never be able to recover from how I handled things. I am so embarrassed.

"Craig, you deserve someone better than me," I say. I'm crying but I mean what I say.

"Don't be ridiculous. Don't underestimate yourself! You just need to get this anxiety, this *painbody*, under control!" he's smiling reassuringly.

"I'm serious. Craig, I'm never going to be able to trust you." I hate admitting it.

"Please stop thinking such negative thoughts. We will work through it together. I know you went through something shit with Sean, but-"

"*Something shit* isn't the words I'd use to describe it. It was awful. It broke me, Craig."

"Babe, I know it did and the fact that something like that happened to *anyone* let alone a woman as incredible as you literally kills me... but you're stronger than this, OK? I see so much strength in you. I am not Sean, I'm not even remotely like him!"

"I know you aren't," I admit, nodding my head but still not meeting his eye. I want to ask him what it is about me that he finds so incredible but I'm afraid of showing him just how non-existent my confidence is.

"So – can we get through this together? Please?"

"I'm always going to be scared, Craig. I'm always going to be careful. I have to be."

He sighs and I look up, chewing the skin from my lip until I can taste blood.

"There's a big difference between being scared and being careful. I can work with careful."

"But you can't work with scared?"

My face contorts as I fight back more tears.

"Regan, you have nothing to be scared of with me. I am never going to hurt you."

Even with the way he is looking at me and the honesty etched into his words, I can't bring myself to believe him. Every guy I have ever dated has said those words to me and every guy had been lying.

"You don't understand. I need you to understand this about me," I beg him, my voice shrill. I'm willing him to understand that I have to keep one step ahead of the game. I have to see things before they happen. I have to protect myself.

"I'm trying to but Regan, the way you're thinking isn't healthy for you or for us. It's not rational," he says.

"Come and sit down," Craig ushers me over to the bar and pours me an orange juice. I am momentarily disappointed that it isn't laced with sparkling wine. Instead of requesting it, I shake away the craving.

My face is in my hands as I apologize. He doesn't say that it's OK, but he rubs the back of my neck reassuringly.

"You've been stressed," he reasons.

"It's more than that, Craig." I'm scared that if I tell him, he won't believe me.

"Talk to me," he says.

I steel myself, swallowing back the bile rising in my throat.

"She slept with Sean."

"She what?" he sounds as though he's had the wind punched out of him. I nod. Just telling someone else about it makes me believe it more.

"That's sick! She's a kid!" he snarls, grabbing two pint glasses and pouring beer from a tap into both. We both down our drinks in silence while he processes what I've told him. I don't tell him that I've been struggling to separate my dreams from reality. It seemed so real. It was real. With him on my side, I believe it.

"If I see that guy people are going to have to hold me back," Craig states matter-of-factly, clenching his jaw. My heart swells.

"Thank you," I say, grateful.

Our eyes lock and we smile at each other.

"I love you." The words slip from my lips before I have a chance to catch them. I gasp, horrified.

"Oh God-" I blush.

"Regan," Craig places his hands back on my arms and steadies me. I look wildly around the bar, anywhere but at him.

"It's soon. It's really soon... but I love you too," he whispers. My head whips up. I feel like I haven't heard those words in years. Sean said them, but he didn't mean them. They sound different now, coming from Craig. They sound real. I find that I believe them.

"I believe you," I say, crying now. I don't think he understands the significance of what I have just said. I've felt unlovable for so long. After finding out about all of the women Sean slept with, I never believed him when he told me he loved me. I didn't believe him when he sat on the edge of our bed and told me how sorry he was while I lay in a ball for three days straight without eating, the blankets in dire need of a wash. I still remember the stale smell in the room, my greasy hair on the limp pillow. I remember feeling like I was the dirty one although I had done nothing wrong.

I didn't believe him when he told me he'd finally realized how much he needed me after being so close to losing me. I didn't believe him when he said those three words, *I love you*, because how could he? He was a narcissist and a liar. He couldn't keep his dick in his pants and I became convinced from that moment on that every man was the same.

I'm not usually one to stereotype but I felt like it was safer to keep everyone at arm's length after that. And now, in the dark and dreary, comforting atmosphere of Craig's bar, I feel the wall I'd built up so high around me start to crumble.

"You should believe me," Craig tells me, breaking me free from my daze.

We lock up the bar and he comes back with me to the cottage.

Harley's bedroom door is closed and I choose not to disturb her.

I find myself touching Craig in the kitchen, my hands on his chest. I trail down his stomach and hips, over his thighs and watch a bulge in his jeans grow. He wants me. I want to please him, to show him how sorry I am for ever having doubted him. I want to claim what is mine and I want Harley to know. She can't have him.

I lead him to my bedroom, already removing particles of clothing.

17

I don't know if I scream because of how deep it is or because my primal instincts want me to mark my territory – either way the sex is fantastic. Craig pushes me onto the bed, allowing me to bounce on the mattress while he unbuckles his belt. I glance over my shoulder, already wet between my legs. When he holds himself and pushes into me, I groan in relief like I've been dying for it all day. Perhaps I have been.

We fuck the way Sean and I once had. I am his to do with as he pleases. I want him to use my body for his pleasure. I want to succumb to what he wants and desires. There is something about the way it had been with Sean that was addictive, unhealthy but so fun. I needed to feel it again. I need Craig to show me he is a man – because to me that's what a man is.

I couldn't tell you when me my own screaming entangled with Harley's. I don't think I'd have noticed if Craig hadn't pulled out of me in a blind panic, his hands slipping over my drenched skin as he pushed away from me.

"What's the matter?" I pant, ears still ringing. It's only then I realized there's screaming coming from somewhere else in the house, not from my mouth.

"Stay here," Craig says, somehow managing to fling a shirt over his head and pull boxers up his legs as he charges into the darkness of the cottage.

I can't hear anything over the sound of Harley's screams and I can't just stay here cowering in the bedroom. I rip my dressing gown from the back of the bathroom door, tearing its label from the neck. I was still trying to wrap it around my otherwise naked body when I run barefoot into the hallway. Unlike Craig, I know where the light switches ae and I put them on as I follow the howling coming from Harley's room. There's no time to think, all I know is I have to get to her. It's strange when you're in a moment like that, life or death. You have no idea what you're going to do, how you're going to think or what you're going to find. I always thought if I was in a situation like this before I'd be smart enough to grab a weapon, or flee and call the police. Instead, I run towards the noise unprepared and unarmed. There was no time to think or prepare.

"Regan, I-" Craig begins. He's outside of her room and wide-eyed. I shove him aside and run towards the screaming. I think I'm expecting the find her with her wrists slit, a bloodied room and a regretful look on her face. I think I'm expecting to find her and know just from looking at her that it's already too late. I think maybe in that dreadful moment, it's what I want to see. I can't differentiate between relief and disappointment when I find her in a ball on the floor. Her face is buried into her knees and her hands are clasped over her ears. She's rocking back and forth, screeching so loud I'm sure the landlord would have called the cops by now.

I race over to her and crouch besides her, trying to unfurl her from her cocoon. She fights me for as long as she can but eventually I'm able to grab her by the wrists. She is perfectly intact, but the veins on her temple look close to bursting. Her corkscrew curls are wet with a combination of sweat and tears. She looked at me like she doesn't know who I am, panic fierce in her eyes. I wonder if she's taken drugs.

"Harley!" I shout above her wails, shaking her by the shoulders. A dusting of recognition seems to come over her as she blinks back her tears, taking in my voice.

"You... you sounded just like she did when she died."

If she had any last shred of self-preservation it's annihilated with those words. She sobs uncontrollably, shaking and mumbling things I can't understand.

When Craig takes a step into the room, her screaming only intensifies.

"What can I do?!" he bellows. I don't know. She seems petrified of him.

"Just go!" I say, my voice probably more irritated than I would like it to sound. Having him go is the last thing I want but I need to calm her down. It breaks my heart to see the hurt in his eyes as he stares down at us. He nods once, taps the door frame with his fist and leaves.

Her screaming subsides the second the front door clicks shut behind him.

I continue to hold her, rocking back and forth on the floorboards with her in my arms. Her breathing slows, hatred seeping through me. I'm in shock, unsure what had set her off or if this was another cry for attention.

She's still muttering something under her breath that I can't make out. I tilt her trembling chin up.

"What are you saying?" I don't know whose heart is beating faster.

"It was him. It was him. It was him." Her words are faint whispers and they make her rock against me faster.

"It was who?!"

My thoughts flash to Craig. What has he done? What is she accusing him of? I hate her. Not Craig. I won't allow her to take away the one good thing in my life. Whatever she is about to say, she's wrong. She has to be.

"It was him. It was him. It was him," her voice raises to a shriek.

My mind races to the night I'd met Craig after Peyton and Nova's funeral. He had tried so hard with me that evening but I'd brushed him off to fuck an older man above the cistern in the pubs bathroom; an older man who hadn't even noticed me and probably didn't even remember me now. I thought of the way Craig had taken me home, ignored my attempts to fuck him that same night. He had come across like the perfect gentleman.

I think of Harley coming up in his Facebook search and his reasonable explanation. It was the perfect answer, almost methodical. I think about my fear in the freezer room, convinced he was locking me in there and my realization that no one would know where I was because our relationship, unbeknownst to me, had remained quite secretive. Why?

I can't believe that Harley was making me think this way.

"It was who, Harley?"

She stares up at me now, her deep brown eyes shimmering with tears. Her pupils are dilated and angry red blood vessels snake over her swollen eyeballs.

"Your father."

*

All of my doubt in Craig suddenly falls away. It has never made any sense no matter how hard I've tried to piece it together. He is a good guy.

Your father...

I think back to his violence and drinking problems, to all of those times I'd been afraid of him. I think of my mother's weakness and fear that for so long I couldn't understand.

He's changed. He's a different man now. I have allowed myself to believe that. I still believe that, don't I?

I think about how Harley never wants to sleep at their house; her unease around all men in general it seems. I register it all, taking it all in too quickly. It's too much.

My dad's grey Nissan X-Trail, the same car seen outside of Peyton's house on the morning of her death. How had I not thought about that before? I guess sometimes you miss what's right in front of you. You block it out, because it couldn't possibly be true.

My dad has changed. He isn't a monster, not anymore.

Your father...

I take one long look at her and spit right in her face.

"You're lying."

18

"Who did this to you?" I ask, my hand touching Peyton's gravestone. I'm alone in the grave yard, Peyton to the left of me, Nova to the right. *Here I am. Stuck in the middle with you.* Stealers Grave is stuck in my head, perhaps the vodka in my hand has something to do with it. I hadn't known where else to go. Craig isn't talking to me. My mother is a drunk and my dad is the latest top pick in the *It Was You* game. So many fingers are getting pointed: Peyton's ex, Craig, my mother, Harley, me and now my dad. The blame has been shifted yet again. Is this what Harley intended? It's like a game of tennis and the overall score is still love-love. I need my best friend, but she's gone.

"It can't be my dad," I tell Peyton through trembling lips, vodka dripping down my chin as I shake my head. It's suddenly so hard to believe my own words. I can't shake the feeling that so much makes sense with it being my father... so much except why? Why would he do it?

Yes he has a history of violence and aggression, but he has changed. Hasn't he? Those bruises I'd passed off as burst blood vessels on my mother's body suddenly make me feel sick. No. Is my mother really so afraid of my father? Is she drinking because it's the only way she knows how to cope? I bring the bottle to my lips and acknowledge that I'm drinking to cope, too. It scares me.

I stay by Peyton and Nova for hours, baking in the African sun and shooing away the Sacred Ibis's lurking around me.

I'm trying to remember everything I possibly can about my father. I've tried so hard to forget the way he had treated me as a little girl. I've worked so hard to let go of the dominance and the drinking; the endless fights, smashed wine glasses, broken doors, holes in the walls. The crying and the fear; the smell of whiskey on his breath so prominent the following day when he'd pretend nothing had happened. All mess had been swept up. Life continued... until the next time. It had taken me such a long time to forgive him, but I had because he had changed. One day it just stopped. Cold turkey. I don't know how or why but he was a changed man.

I think of all of the stories he's told me in the past about his time involved in the war in Saudi Arabia; the place in the Middle East that had eaten his soul. I remember the look in his eyes when he had told me one night after too much whiskey that he'd killed people before. It was a look of regret, of self-hatred.

He couldn't have killed someone. Not again. He couldn't.

I remembered how his eyes had brimmed with tears as he'd told me how he'd thought of the parents of those he'd shot at point-blank range.

I tried to imagine myself in his shoes; holding a gun, fighting for my country. Pointing a gun at someone, knowing I was about to end their life. I couldn't.

"I have to ask him," I whisper to Peyton's grave. I snivel into my sleeve, the grass itchy on my bare knees as I pull myself up. Withered protea petals brush against my feet in the breeze.

My phone buzzes. Craig again.

What happened? Is everything alright?

I've been ignoring him since he left the cottage. What could I say to him? *'Oh well, turns out my dad's a murderer. Sorry I ever doubted you by the way!'* It sounds ridiculous.

I pocket my phone, wishing for once that life could just be normal. I leave the graveyard with a sense of dread, scared of what I'm about to learn about my father.

◊

"Dad," I croak, standing in the doorway of my family home. I'm crying already.

"Darling, what's the matter?"

He looks genuinely concerned and that makes this harder. I flinch away as he tries to reach out to me. My rock, my confidant, how could I ask him this? He hadn't been there for me when I was a baby, an infant or even a teenager, but he's made up for it in my later years. I remembered all of the times I'd called him above anyone else when I was upset in Spain, how I'd cried down the phone and how his voice had soothed me. I remembered how he'd helped me out financially when I had needed to book a flight out of Mallorca because Sean had kept all of my credit cards from me. I remembered the way he had welcomed me back home with open arms when I'd needed it. Not all dads would do that. I'd always thought my dad would be the kind of father who would make you learn the hard way; make you dig your own way out of the messy situations you end up in... but he always did what he could to help me.

Did you kill Peyton?

What did you do to her, dad?

Dad, I need you to tell me the truth...

Nothing feels quite right on the tongue.

"Harley-" I start, but he interrupts me.

"What's happened? Is she OK?" he asks, too quickly.

Why is he so concerned for her?

Why does he care about her so much?

It makes me cry harder.

"She told me you did it, dad. She said you killed Peyton."

I watch as my father drops his head.

My heart falls.

The silence would have been endless had I not broken it.

"Why?" my voice is shaking.

Absolutely everything around me seems to disappear. My senses fail me. The smell of meat sizzling on the grill, the hiss of fat seeping from sausages, our home with all of its imperfections all seem to fall away from me as everything goes black.

I have to be dreaming.

This isn't real.

I will myself to wake up.

"I wanted to give you a family," his whispered words snap me back to the present. His eyes are cast down toward the ground.

I don't understand.

Every molecule of hatred I had long since buried for my father resurfaces.

"It was you," I sob.

19

"You are going to rot in jail like you were meant to a long time ago!" The words I had screeched to my father still echo in my head.

His response, nodding like he agreed, swigging the whiskey in his hand is all that I can see.

"Take care of your mother, OK?" he'd asked me as the handcuffs were put tightly around his wrists. They were the last words my dad said to me. He didn't look sad or hurt or scared, it was as though he had seen this all coming.

I'd called the police on my father.

I'd sent him away to a life in prison.

I'd promised him that he would never see me again.

When I was younger I could never have imagined having someone other than my mother as my best friend, particularly not my father. But that is what he had become to me over the years. My best friend.

"Thank you, Regan," Harley cried into my neck, holding onto me like her life depended on it. She keeps saying it, sounding so grateful and pleased that the man responsible for her mother's murder has now been locked away. As though that changes anything. It doesn't.

Nothing can bring Peyton back... or my dad.

"I didn't want to tell you that it was your dad. I didn't want to hurt you. I was so scared every time we went there."

I can't respond to her.

I can't move.

I stay frozen to the spot, knowing time won't stop regardless of my begging it to.

Nothing. Feels. Real.

I want to tell Harley that I'm sorry for ever having doubted her, but I can't do it. I swallow it back.

She had known all along that my father had killed her mother. I had put her in the same room as him on countless occasions. How had I not felt something? I've always had an uncanny intuition. I always know when something isn't right, even throughout the entire relationship with Sean I had known something was going on. My instincts were never wrong.

My dad murdered my best friend. For me. No. It isn't right. It doesn't fit – but his confession proves otherwise. It's there in black and white, in full detail. Even as I hold the two-sided piece of paper in my hands and try to read it back to myself I can't bring myself to believe it or understand.

'It became apparent to me recently that my daughter, Regan Pen, was never going to keep a relationship going with a man long enough for it to progress into marriage and children. I realized that

she was lonely. I needed to rectify that.'

I bite down onto my knuckles and I sob. In many ways he's right. I'm already trying to sabotage my relationship with Craig before it can get too serious.

I eventually went to the bar, two bottles of wine lining my stomach. I laugh at my mundane routine as I lock my car in the parking lot. I'm either always at the cottage searching for a nonexistent job or shopping at the local supermarket or at Craig's bar. That's my life. I guess when you live in such a small town you don't have the luxury of choice. It isn't like the cities, Cape Town, Durban or Johannesburg, where you're spoiled for choice with where to go. I used to think that was the beauty of small towns; that comforting feeling of knowing everyone, being familiar with your surroundings. Now I feel trapped.

He doesn't look happy to see me when I walk in. I order a vodka tonic and he asks me if I'm sure I need another drink.

"I haven't been drinking," I lie. I can't read the expression on his face as he stares back at me.

I down the drink quickly, sweating the alcohol out into my clothes and hair. My skin is damp and drained of color. I slam a clammy palm onto the counter, making the patrons around me jump.

"We need to talk!" I demand. Even through my hazy vision I can see Craig working his jaw.

"This isn't the time or the place, Regan. I'm working."

I bring the empty glass up to my lips and slam it down onto the counter in anger when I realize there's nothing in it. The glass cracks. I don't know where all of the aggression is coming from. "Oh right. You're too busy for me, aren't you?! There are so many other important things for you to do, like your *job*!" I spit. I feel suddenly furious that I'm still unemployed.

Craig snatches the broken glass from my grip and tosses it into a plastic bin with other broken glasses and empty bottles.

I look around me, anger flooding through me for no good reason. There's an ashtray to my left and I pick it up, it's full of ash and cigarette butts. I toss it at him from across the bar.

"We're done!" I say.

People around me start gathering up their belongings and shuffle away from me.

The room is cloudy with so much ash that I can barely make out when Craig comes around to the other side of the bar and grabs me by the scruff of my neck.

My body feels like jelly as he pulls me outside and throws me into the parking lot.

"I'll put your car keys in your letter box in the morning. Get out of here and don't come back," he gives me a filthy look before heading back into the bar.

"Craig! Please. I'm sorry. I don't know what came over me. I'm just – I'm going through some stuff!" I say, running after him.

"There's always something with you, isn't there?" he's shaking his head at me. He smelled like an ashtray.

"Craig, please?" I started to cry as I reach out to touch him. He pulls away.

"Go home."

So I do.

I haven't even had the chance to tell him about my father. I haven't known how. This rage has possessed me. It isn't who I am. I'm scaring myself. I walked home in the dark, sobbing, knowing that the only thing to be scared of right now is myself.

I still haven't told anyone about my father. I don't want anyone to know. It's going to come out eventually anyway. It'll be in the papers and the entire town will know who really killed Peyton. I'll have to leave again. I'll never be able to show my face in public. So I ended things with Craig. It's what I always do. I run away.

That strange first night back in my bed, I've never felt more alone. Harley is with my mother. I need time to myself. It feel as though my father has just died, too. I'm in mourning.

I look at my Facebook page, the bright screen caning my eyes in the darkness.

My dad's words reverberate off of the walls. I look at all of my old girlfriends that I haven't reached out to in months and see how happy they seemed in their relationships. In their lives. They don't have a world thriving on drama like mine. They're settled. They're happy. I can no longer ask myself why they have that and I don't. The answer is all around me.

They don't focus on the negative things the way that I do or get caught up in the smallest things that their boyfriends don't do. They get on with things. They don't spend their evenings strangling the neck of a bottle of wine in their hand. They don't sneak into their partner's private messages and try to find something to prove that they are a lying sack of shit. They are just content. I don't think I've ever really known what that word means.

I do wonder if nothing bad has ever happened to them or if they just know how to deal with things better than I do. Everyone has something going on with them, don't they? It just seems like there is 'always something' with me. That's what Craig had said that night outside of the bar. He's right, of course.

I lay there in the darkness and silence, wishing I could understand myself and my fight or flight way of surviving.

I cry myself to sleep after deleting my Facebook profile. I don't want to measure my life up against anyone else's anymore.

20

"Going to such extremities to ease your loneliness is the actions of someone who is deeply disturbed, Regan. You need to know that and accept that this isn't your fault. Your father has a long history with mental illness that no one was aware of. He was not in control of himself."

I've started seeing a new therapist. I'm his pro bono case.

He's told me that I'm still in the denial stage of grief and that it's normal. I tell him it can't have been my dad, that I don't believe it. I tell him that something isn't right. Something isn't adding up. He let me talk. He listened.

◊

I'd come in shaking with nerves, not knowing where to start. *From the beginning*, he'd said. So I did. I told him my life story from the alcoholism that runs deep in my family's veins, my history with anxiety, depression and self-harm, my love for a bottle of wine every evening. I tried passing it off as a glass, but he saw past me. "You don't need to be afraid to be yourself here, Regan. This is for me to better understand you and help you."

I speak to him about my mother and my fears of becoming exactly like her. I wanted him to tell me that would never happen, but he nods and agrees with me that it is happening. Like mother like daughter.

I speak to him about Sean, about how he'd cheated on me and I'd stayed. I tell him how feeling desired by a man that had strayed from me so much to be with other women actually turned me on. I tell him how I like knowing I can still be so powerful with my body. He told me that Sean had never thought of my body as a powerful tool the way that I had. He'd told me Sean had thought of my body as a play thing. I realized that he had. He had. He had. He had.

I cried three sessions in. Sean had always had the ability to break me. I could keep cold and strong when it came to my family problems, but Sean always shredded me apart.

I tell the therapist about my thoughts of dropping the toaster into the bathtub or cutting my wrists with the pizza cutter. I tell him how I know I would never really do those things but that the thoughts are there and that they scare me. I tell him about how there had been a time when I would have done things like that and that I didn't know how I'd gotten through it. He reminds me that the point is that I had gotten through it. He reminds me that I'll get through this, too, because I'm stronger than I realize..

That night I went home and sat cross-legged in front of my full length mirror, watching myself as I polished off a bottle of the cheapest wine I could find in the liquor store. Gone were the days where I would spend money on one excessively delicious bottle of Shiraz from one of the wine regions best vineyards. I bought and drank too much wine now and couldn't afford to have such high standards anymore.

My mother's eyes stare back at me in the mirror. My dad's features shine through. Hollow cheeks, long nose, prominent jaw-line that trembles as I see them both in my reflection. I'm noticing things.

In the next session we speak about Peyton. We speak about our friendship over the years and what it had meant to me. We speak about my guardianship and how I had pushed Harley away since day one. We speak about my dad's confession and how I refuse to visit him in jail. I tell him how I hate myself for missing him and loving him even after learning about what he's done. He reassures me that it's normal to feel this way because regardless of what he's done, he will always be my father; my father that I hate, my father that I never want to see again – my father that I will always love and will miss every single day for the rest of my life.

I continue to see him, confiding in him about all sorts of things that suddenly seem like a relief to get off of my chest. We speak about my trust issues. We speak about my relationship with Craig and how because of what Sean had done to me I can't bring myself to be truly happy with him. We speak about the way I constantly measure myself up against all of the tight-arsed Argentinian, Brazilian and Spanish sluts that look ten times better in a bikini than I ever could. The ones that Sean had cheated on me with. We speak about me calling them sluts when technically *they* had done nothing wrong. We speak about the fact that I refuse to do any exercise to help me on the 'bikini bod' front. We speak about my body issues, about how I have seen my body change so much in the past year and how I'm not sure if it is just because I'm getting older or if it's because I let myself go after Sean. He tells me it's both. He tells me it sounds like I'm not respecting my body or myself anymore because Sean had never respected me. He tells me that I don't believe I deserve respect. He's right.

I go home after that session and lace up my Nikes. I go for a run around the lagoon. It's more of an exasperated walk requiring my inhaler than a real run, but it's a step in the right direction.
I find myself at the graveyard and by now I can find Peyton's spot blindfolded. I brush a cobweb from her name and stroke her gravestone lovingly. I tell her how sorry I am for what happened to her even though I still don't quite believe it. I make a promise to her to be a good mother to Harley even though I still don't want to be. She's my responsibility now.

That night I treat myself to one glass of wine and cuddle the cat on the sofa after calling Harley and my mother to see if they were getting on alright. I promise them I'll see them soon.

After finishing the call I type in Craig's number. I miss him so much that every part of me aches.

'There's always something with you...' he'd said. His words cut me deep, down to the grit of my bones. I'd staggered out of his bar, slamming the door behind me with a terrible aggression that I hadn't seem coming. The booze was changing me. It was giving me the aggression I had seen so often in my father and it was killing me, destroying my mind and taking a hold of me just like it had done with my mother. It wouldn't let go. I hated it but I loved it. I was addicted.

You were right.

I text him. His response, as always, is speedy.

It's been so long since seeing a new message pop up on my phone from him. I stare at it, unopened, for a while. This is what I want. I want to get messages for him. I want him to come over and to be there for me. I want to be there for him, too.

I open the message.

?

I draw in a breath. I guess a part of me is scared that it's already too late. Will he even want me anymore? Since we'd started this thing with us I had been a wreck. I'd been shagging some stranger in his bathroom, drunk most of the nights that I'd been with him. I'd gone into his phone and invaded his privacy, accused him of being a pedophile and thought that he was planning to murder me in his freezer. He knows I can't trust him and that I'm still scared he'll turn out to be just like Sean because my hope in man-kind has whittled itself down to nothing.

How can he still want me? What can I say to show him how sorry I am and that things would be different now?

Please come over.

I reply, and then I wait.

I wait and I wait and I wait. Five minutes pass, then ten.

Maybe he's already driving here. I nod to myself, knowing that's the case.

My ears prick up at every sound of a car hurtling by my driveway, relief floods over me that he's here, but none of the cars pull in.

It takes me over three hours to realize that he isn't coming… and even then I carry on waiting.

At about four AM I drag myself out of bed. I can't sleep. My eyes are puffy and swollen, my nose blocked and I smell bad. I walk into the kitchen and boil the kettle. There's a bottle of wine on the counter, staring at me. I look at it while the kettle vibrates angrily on its holder. I pick it up and untwist the cap, smelling its fruity flavors. I close it again, inhale deeply and throw the full bottle into the bin.

Sacrilege, a part of my mind screams at me, begging me to recover it.

Necessary, reassures another as I walk zombie-like across the room. I snip the tip from a hazelnut latte sachet and pour the contents into my favorite mint green mug. I can't remember when I had last really *enjoyed* a cup of coffee.

I hold the steaming mug in my hand and bring it over to my laptop with me. I open up a blank Word document and begin to write.

Dear Craig,

I hope you're well… I'm so sorry that I drove you away. I'm so sorry that things have been so crazy with us so early in our relationship. It breaks my heart that it's ruined us already. All of this breaks my heart. I have never felt as alone as I do right now, sitting here in my pajamas sobbing my heart out.

The cottage feels empty without you.

I messaged you last night begging you to come over because I missed you so much and then I kept hearing cars outside and I kept getting this flood of relief thinking you were coming in. If you had I would have just run into your arms and apologized and told you how sorry I am... because I know things need to change and I know I need help with my drinking. I'm seeing someone new now, a therapist who is going to help me with all of that and everything else too. I just needed you to know that.

I know you've been trying your best to help and to understand and I'm sorry I have made everything so awful for you...

I'm just so lost right now and I have so much anger inside of me about so many things. I've been under a lot of pressure to make it work here, to get a good job, look after Harley, deal with my best friend's death and so much more that you don't even know about while still trying to work through what happened with Sean. I'm trying so hard to keep it together and find a happy place and I feel like I'm failing.

All this pressure building up around me made me crumble the other night in your bar. I never should have acted the way I did or disrespected your property. I disrespected you and for that I am so sorry.

I need you. I really want you and I love you. I know that things need to change and I really am making an effort to make that happen.

My new therapist is wonderful. There are tears falling onto the keyboard as I type this. I didn't want to admit that I needed help with my drinking. I don't want to feel weak – and that's why I fight so much… because I'm trying so hard to be strong when I am probably the weakest, coldest person in the world right now.

I am so angry with life and I don't really know where to start explaining things or how to explain them in a way that works…

My heart is broken about my father – it's come out that he killed Peyton, Craig. I didn't know how to tell you because it changes everything. No one else knows yet and I'd really appreciate it if you keep it to yourself for the time being. It's going to come out soon enough… but that's why I was the way that I was the other night. I tipped over the edge because I'd just found out my dad had murdered my best friend.

Do you want to know why???

For ME! That was his reasoning.

He said that he thought I was lonely and he wanted to help.

My best friend is dead because of me… because I couldn't make a relationship work in my life and be happy.

It's destroyed me. The therapist tells me it isn't my fault but how can it not be? My dad felt like I would never have a family of my own so he took matters into his own hands. I still don't believe it.

Why couldn't he have just suggested adoption or spoken to me about it? I don't understand how he came to the idea of murdering Peyton! It just doesn't add up and something feels SO wrong with it but his confession is there. He did it... for the most absurd reason I have ever heard. The therapist said he has obviously been mentally unstable for many years and keeps reminding me that it isn't my fault. But it is.

But I guess I need to tell you about the other things, too. About why I have been drinking so much even before Peyton was killed and my dad was put in jail.

I guess my drinking started mainly because of my mother. I'm heart-broken over her, Craig. She's dying. I don't even know if she's going to make it to the end of this year and I keep trying so hard to be strong about it but I'm not OK. We used to be so close. We used to be best friends... and I know now that one day if I ever get married she won't be there. Even if she is alive by the time that ever happens, she won't be there in the way that I need her to be. I know I shouldn't be thinking about marriage and babies and all that shit yet because we are new but I do. When I get into a relationship with someone I like to think I know where the relationship will go... but I'll talk about that later.

I feel like my mother is already dead and that I'm going through grief. I'm angry at my family for not forcing her to get the help she needs. I'm embarrassed by them all and I hate that when people ask me how they are I don't know what to say. I feel like a disappointment to you. I wish I had a normal, loving happy family that I could be proud of but I don't. I want one so badly and I want to build one of my own and make it everything that my family isn't... that's another reason I think about the future so much. I'm trying so hard and striving towards making this the thing that I have always missed. I desperately want a good, loving family....Things will never be normal in my family and I feel like a burden to you because of it. That's why I never want to talk about it with you. But I'm lonely because they are all I know and all I have... and regardless of who they are and how much I do hate them, I love them too... because they are the only family I have.

I tried so hard to find 'my place' in the world where things felt right. I could never find it. I've never really known where I belong. I don't have that sense of belonging and peace of mind that I am where I am meant to be – I didn't, until now. You're it. You're who I want the world with, Craig. I guess all this time I've been fighting it and not sure about it, trying to find ways to cock it up and sabotage it because I'm so afraid of getting hurt again. I'm pushing you and forcing us into negative spaces because if it's good and if I'm happy, I'm scared I will get hurt. I'm so scared of that. If you hurt me I don't know how I'll recover and I hate putting that pressure on you but I *don't know how to trust you won't disappoint me the way that every single other person has in my life!!! Just the thought of it sends me into a panic.*

Every time I think I'm where I'm supposed to be, it gets ripped away from me.... That is why I think about the future so much now. I never used to be like this and I wish you had known me before. I trusted, I lived and I loved unconditionally. There was never any drama or fights. I miss that version of me so much and I want her back, for me and for you.

There is so much stuff from my past that I need to deal with to be able to move forward in life. Sean is a huge part of that. Because of him I find it so difficult to trust you. I guess I push you because I think one day you'll crack and something will come up to make you just like him. I'll find out you've been talking to other women or cheating on me or you'll hit me... I don't know. He's really fucked me up and it is hard for me to believe that you really are as amazing as you are.

Craig... I know this is my fault. The way we are now is because of how I handled things. How I reacted was terrible and I know that... I just have so much anger inside of me and fear and nerves... I need to deal with the things from my past to be able to accept love and happiness again...

Please take me back. Please try to understand why I have been the way I have and know that from here on in things will be so different.

I will never disrespect you again.

You're it for me.

I love you.

Regan xx

By the time I've finished and hit send my coffee is cold and I'm exhausted. I go to bed and sleep for hours.

21

I guess I'm feeling so good after that email, after sharing all of my feelings with Craig, that I'm sure I'll wake up to a reply. When I eventually get up and refresh my inbox to find nothing, I don't understand.

A part of me wants to email him again and tell him I know that how I acted was terrible and I really am going to change... but I've already said that. I don't know what else I can say.

So I decide to shut my laptop, pick up the phone and call Harley.

"Come home," I tell her.

While my mother drives her over I freshen up her room. I take the creases out of her bed and draw open the curtains, shedding light into the room that had frightened me since the day she moved in. It's time to move past that now. It's time to be her mother.

◊

Craig replies two days later. I'm in the kitchen dropping rosemary sprigs into the crockpot. Harley's tapping her pencil against the tabletop as she works on her math homework and I'm trying desperately hard to pretend that it isn't annoying me.

When my phone chimes and Craig's name comes up, my back goes taut. It feels like someone has ripped out my stomach.

"Regan, you OK?" Harley asks, looking up at me from her textbook.

"Yeah! Just give me a moment," I wink.

We've been getting on so well over the past two days and it really feels like we're starting to understand each other better.

The therapist told me that now she has closure over her mother's murder it would be so much easier for Harley to move on. It really seems that way. She's so at peace and friendly with me. It's like a different girl is in my house.

I walk into my room and shut the door behind me. My hand shakes as I unlock the phone and I don't know if it's the nerves from seeing what Craig had to say or if it's once again from the lack of booze. Either way I haven't touched a drop of alcohol for over forty-eight hours. I have a long way to go but I'm getting there.

I open his message, unprepared for whatever it contains.

Dear Regan,

I'm not much of a writer… so please bear with me.

Since I have been with you things have been so taxing. This has all just all hit me so hard – it's very scary and not at all a good sign that we are this bad so early in our relationship.

We have a long way to go for us to be truly happy together so all of this needs to be worked out quickly. You want the things that most couples have after years of being together and they will often say 'oh yeah gee the first year, that was the best, that was the honeymoon period' - things generally only get harder after that and relationships are truly tested so I think you really need to cool your jets and make sure you're truly happy and this is what you really want, or this will be over before we ever really get traction. I need you to understand all this and really digest it.

Having all this shit going on while I'm working cannot happen. I know you're still looking for a job and you can't think much of someone who just owns a bar but that bar is my life so for you to come in and disrespect it really hurt me. I need you to understand the full gravitational impact of your behavior and that it will not be tolerated, ever.

I will use this moment now to say that if you ever say and do those things again then we are over – honestly – I will not be sworn at, I will not be told we're over or done. That is not what people who love and respect each other do! We are meant to want the best for each other in every way, to really amplify what makes each of us special and unique and for that to shine through always. That's what people normally really adore about each other and makes the relationship special and bonding.

You need to reconnect with your old friends, Regan. I can't be the only person you have in your life. I can't be your everything. I know *that things have been hard for you since you lost Peyton but you*

need to start moving forward...and I can't, no, I WON'T have you

doubting us – I have done nothing but love and support you and this

fear you have because of Sean... it's toxic to any relationship and

breeds doubt that will ruin us!!! Our relationship clearly has not got

the maturity and stability I need, so for us to have any chance of a

future together this all needs to be clearly understood with a plan in

place to ensure it will never happen again or we will be done,

instantly.

I thank you for really opening up to me, that's really brave and I

appreciate it. I'm sorry for not writing back to you sooner. Like I

said, I'm not much of a writer and I needed this to really portray

everything I am thinking and feeling. To be honest Regan, I'm

hurting.

I have always had the motto in life to keep things simple and have

fun. The world is so crazy a lot of the time and I find it unhealthy to

get caught up it in all. That said, I am happy to talk to you about the

future at the right time but I do think you're trying to put way too

much pressure on us far too early in our relationship. I think you

worry about things too much.

Moving on I want to mention this really interesting book I have *started reading and struggling to put down - The Subtle Art Of Not Giving A F*ck by Mark Manson.*

It's bizarre that I find this book at this time and it's so weird reading it because there are just so many home truths in it and I highly recommend you read it — only a couple pages in it just hit me with him talking about how people in today's society care way to much about way too many things, I think you should read this a couple times like I have. To quote: "The problem is that giving too many fucks is bad for your mental health. It causes you to become overly attached to the superficial and fake, to dedicate your life to chasing a mirage of happiness and satisfaction. The key to a good life is not giving a fuck about more, it's giving a fuck about less, giving a fuck about only what is true and immediate and important".

I think you can see why that hit me with a lot of things I have been trying to say to you and seems relevant to about 95% of what you said in your email. Only a couple chapters in and there's just quote after quote of relevance to you and I. There is a section on the Feedback Loop from Hell which I think you would really understand around the brain and how it works with anxiety and anger to stress and guilt.

It's hard to hear you talk about your mother and father like that — I obviously can't pretend to know what it's like, other than to say I'm here for you, my family and friends are here for you, I love you and I'm proud of you and we are your family. I didn't want to make the thing with your dad the main focus of this email because it isn't the main focus of you and me. You are not your family, Regan... and I am not going to leave you because your mother is an alcoholic and your dad is a murderer. I will leave you if you keep drinking the way that you do – I think you know more than anyone what it does to the people around you if you go down that path!? Don't do that to me.

I am your rock – just make sure you keep me by your side or at least in your pocket going forward. Don't try to throw me or skim me across the ocean for us to sink alone.

It might be odd coming from an old boxing movie but I have to admit the quote from the movie Rocky has always stuck with me: "You, me, or nobody is gonna hit as hard as life. But it ain't about how hard ya hit. It's about how hard you can get hit and keep moving forward. How much you can take and keep moving forward. That's how winning is done!"

I love you and know we can rebuild this relationship, I'll see you tomorrow to start a-fresh – what do ya say?

Craig xx

I have to read his email a few times over to really make sure he hasn't giving up on me, to believe that this is real.

I vow then to change, to seek the help I need to get back to a good place where I can love and trust and be myself again. I will no longer allow Sean to control my life. I think I've said that to myself so many times in the past but I never really meant it. I do now. I really do now.

I walk back out into the kitchen and place my hands onto Harley's shoulders.

"How's the math coming along?" I ask her, and I find myself genuinely caring.

Her smile fills the room, her eyes bright; boring right into mine.

"Fine, thanks, Regan. Will dinner be ready soon?"

I smile back at her, even though there's still a little something off-putting about the look in her eyes.

I ease my hands beneath soapy water filling the sink and look over at the crockpot exuding the most delicious smells of rosemary and lamb.

"Just a few more minutes," I tell her, not quite aware that I am slipping nicely into the motherhood role already.

Epilogue

I'd known I'd chosen wisely when I'd picked Regan's dad to take the fall.

I could tell that he was selfless right from the start. He was always trying to please others. Grovel. It sickened me; his need for redemption, atoning for his sins… but he was also, ostensibly, exactly what I had needed.

I knew he'd cover for me if I played my cards the right way. There was no way he would let a young girl spend the rest of her life in jail, being known as a killer. After I'd told him my story I knew he wouldn't let that happen to me.

"You've been through more than enough already," I knew he would say. And he had. His predictability was a luxury I hadn't seen coming. Not until I'd gotten to know him.

"I killed Peyton," I'd said to him as he'd clutched onto his whiskey, making him rehearse.

"I killed Peyton. Say it until it sounds real," I'd ordered, staring into his eyes. Sullying his lips with lies was empowering.

It wasn't like I was a bad person. Not really. Yes, I drove a knife into my mother's stomach and yes I killed her but everything I had done had been for *her*. For Nova. I hadn't meant to kill *her*. She had been collateral damage... as they say. I'd really only ever wanted to help her.

I couldn't allow my mother to do the things she had done to me to my baby sister.

My mother didn't deserve another child. My mother deserved to be dead. That's why I chopped off every one of her disgusting, fat fingers and pointed them directly at herself. She was to blame for all of this. Those filthy fingers that touched me in places your mother should never touch you.

I had reveled in the acrid stench of her blood all around me that night and I had screamed not from sadness or fear but from relief. She would never hurt me again. The woman that everyone loved and adored, the woman that was nothing more than a liar... gone. I was glad. I was free.

She had ruined me. I like to think that my actions were permissible, even if no one else would think so too.

I chew at my nails as I stare down at my textbook, brushing my fingers down the sheaf of mind-numbing papers. Sunlight filtered through the blinds, casting the soft peach of sunset onto my page. The blustery day was coming to an end, winter stealing us from autumn far too soon. The crockpot had been dusted off already and was currently home to two meaty lamb shanks cooking under a bubbling red sauce.

I tear a piece of my nail off and crunch it beneath my teeth. I can still taste the blood on my tongue if I try. I lick my lips and smile at Regan, for we are bound by Peyton now, forever.

Acknowledgements

I am so grateful to everyone who has always believed in me and my dream to be a writer. I'm blessed with so many amazing people in my life who support my ambitions and want to help me achieve my goals. There's honestly too many of you to name but you know who you are and YOU are the people who helped make this possible.

Thank you to my incredible partner, Mark Sheather, for allowing me to ramble on about my ideas and for reading my early drafts. You always offer me advice and are always trying to make my work the best it can be – you even put up with me when I jump the gun and get too excited and spontaneous. You're the love of my life.

Thank you to Michelle Shelby (or should I say Grant?!) for reading the first few chapters early on too and for making me feel so good about my work. Your positivity and feedback is so appreciated.

Thank you to my dad who has always read everything I've ever written and stayed up with me at all hours of the night talking about book ideas over bottles of wine and whiskey. You've always given me constructive criticism and have never sugar coated anything for me. You taught me to work hard and to never give up.

Thank you also to Andrew Hoare in Brisbane at The Illustrators, for the incredible cover design! It's gorgeous and I couldn't be happier with it.

Lastly, thank you to the people who buy my books, read it, reach out to me – review it on Goodreads or other platforms and help me grow as a writer.

Please remember that alcoholism is a very serious illness that creeps up on you over time. If you are concerned that either you or a loved one is in danger of this addiction please contact your local alcohol support group.

The moment you catch yourself saying you 'need' a drink is the moment you need to realize you have a problem and fix it before you lose yourself and everyone that you love.

Made in the USA
Monee, IL
04 January 2020

19865608R00129